Finding Father Christmas

Finding Father Christmas

Robin Jones Gunn

Faith Words

NEW YORK   BOSTON   NASHVILLE

With thanks to R. W. Crump and Louisiana State University Press for their work on *The Complete Poems of Christina Rossetti*, volume one of which includes the text of "A Christmas Carol," here quoted as "My Gift."

FaithWords
Hachette Book Group USA
237 Park Avenue
New York, NY 10017
Visit our Web site at www.faithwords.com.

Book design by Fearn Cutler de Vicq
Printed in the United States of America
FIRST EDITION: OCTOBER 2007
10 9 8 7 6 5 4 3 2 1

FaithWords is a division of Hachette Book Group USA, Inc.
The FaithWords name and logo is a trademark of Hachette Book Group USA, Inc.

Library of Congress Cataloging-in-Publication Data
Gunn, Robin Jones
Finding Father Christmas / Robin Jones Gunn. — 1st ed.
        p. cm.
Summary: "A poignant Christmas novella about a woman, desperate for a place to belong, who finds herself in London a few days before Christmas, looking for the father she never knew"—Provided by the publisher
ISBN-13: 978-0-446-52629-6
ISBN-10: 0-446-52629-0
1. Fathers and daughters—Fiction. 2. London
(England)—Fiction. 3. Christmas stories. I. Title.
PS3557.U4866F56 2007
813'.54—dc22   2007009629

For Rachel and Stephanie,
who made our jaunt to London an absolute delight.

Acknowledgments

A round of warm thank-yous to my British friends: Penny and Anna Culliford, who showed me the Kent countryside and introduced me to English pudding; Marion Stroud, who opened to me her heart and home and gave valuable feedback for the story; and Heather Thomas, who recognized the Christina Rossetti Christmas poem when she read the first draft of this manuscript—and then sang the poem for me as she did when she was a child. A forever thank you to my husband, Ross Gunn III; to my agent, Janet Kobobel Grant; and to my blue-beach-chair-sister, Anne deGraaf. Each of you infused this little book with your encouragement and support. Many thanks to Rolf Zettersten, Chip MacGregor, Anne Goldsmith, and the entire team at FaithWords.

Finding Father Christmas

"Come in! Come in, and know me better."

—Spirit of Christmas Present
from *A Christmas Carol* by Charles Dickens

Chapter One

A string of merry silver bells jumped and jingled as the north wind shook the evergreen wreath on the heavy wooden door. Overhead a painted shingle swung from two metal arms, declaring this place of business to be the Tea Cosy.

As I peered inside through the thick-paned window, I could see a cheerful amber fire in the hearth. Tables were set for two with china cups neatly positioned on crimson tablecloths. Swags of green foliage trimmed the mantel. Dotted across the room, on the tables and on shelves, were a dozen red votive candles. Each tiny light flickered, sending out promises of warmth and cheer, inviting me to step inside.

Another more determined gust made a swoop down the lane, this time taking my breath with it into the darkness of the December night.

This trip was a mistake. A huge mistake. What was I thinking?

I knew the answer as it rode off on the mocking wind. The answer was, I wasn't thinking. I was feeling.

Pure emotion last Friday nudged me to book the round-trip ticket to London. Blind passion convinced me that the answer to my twenty-year question would be revealed once I reached the Carlton Photography Studio on Bexley Lane.

Sadly, I was wrong. I had come all this way only to hit a dead end.

I took another look inside the teahouse and told myself to keep walking, back to the train station, back to the hotel in London where I had left my luggage. This exercise in futility was over. I might as well change my ticket and fly back to San Francisco in the morning.

My chilled and weary feet refused to obey. They wanted to go inside and be warmed by the fire. I couldn't deny that my poor legs did deserve a little kindness after all I had put them through when I folded them into the last seat in coach class. The middle seat, by the lavatories, in the row that didn't recline. A cup of tea at a moment like this might be the only blissful memory I would take with me from this fiasco.

Reaching for the oddly shaped metal latch on the door, I stepped inside and set the silver bells jingling again.

"Come in, come in, and know me better, friend!" The unexpected greeting came from a kilt-wearing man with a valiant face. His profoundly wide sideburns had the look of white lamb's wool and softened the resoluteness in his jaw. "Have you brought the snowflakes with you, then?"

"The snowflakes?" I repeated.

"Aye! The snowflakes. It's cold enough for snow, wouldn't you say?"

I nodded my reluctant agreement, feeling my nose and cheeks going rosy in the small room's warmth. I assumed the gentleman who opened the door was the proprietor. Looking around, I asked, "Is it okay if I take the table by the fire? All I'd like is a cup of tea."

"I don't see why not. Katharine!" He waited for a response and then tried again. "Katharine!"

No answer came.

"She must have gone upstairs. She'll be back around." His grin was engaging, his eyes clear. "I would put the kettle on for you myself, if it weren't for the case of my being on my way out at the moment."

"That's okay. I don't mind waiting."

"Of course you don't mind waiting. A young woman such as yourself has the time to wait, do you not? Whereas, for a person such as myself . . ." He leaned closer and with a wink confided in me, "I'm Christmas Present, you see. I can't wait."

What sort of "present" he supposed himself to be and to whom, I wasn't sure.

With a nod, the man drew back the heavy door and strode into the frosty air.

From a set of narrow stairs a striking woman descended. She looked as surprised at my appearance as I was at hers. She wore a stunning red, floor-length evening dress. Around her neck hung a sparkling silver necklace, and dangling from under her dark hair were matching silver earrings. She stood tall with careful posture and tilted her head, waiting for me to speak.

"I wasn't sure if you were still open."

"Yes, on an ordinary day we would be open for another little while, until five thirty. . . ." Her voice drifted off.

"Five thirty," I repeated, checking my watch. The time read 11:58. The exact time I'd adjusted it to when I had deplaned at Heathrow Airport late that morning. I tapped on the face of my watch as if that would make it run again. "I can see you have plans for the evening and that you're ready to close. I'll just—"

"Che-che-che." The sound that came from her was the sort used to call a squirrel to come find the peanuts left for it on a park bench. It wasn't a real word from a real language, but I understood the meaning. I was being invited to stay and not to run off.

"Take any seat you want. Would you like a scone with your tea or perhaps some rum cake?"

"Just the tea, thank you."

I moved toward the fire and realized that a scone sounded pretty good. I hadn't eaten anything since the undercooked breakfast omelet served on the plane.

"Actually, I would like to have a scone, too. If it's not too much trouble."

"No trouble at all."

Her smile was tender, motherly. I guessed her to be in her midfifties or maybe older. She turned without any corners or edges to her motions. I soon heard the clinking of dishes as she prepared the necessary items in the kitchen.

Making my way to a steady looking table by the fire, I tried to tuck my large shoulder bag under the spindle leg of the chair. The stones along the front of the hearth were permanently blackened from what I imagined to be centuries of soot. The charm of the room increased as I sat down and felt the coziness of the close quarters. This was a place of serenity. A place where trust between friends had been established and kept for many years.

A sense of safety and comfort called to the deepest part of

my spirit and begged me to set free a fountain of tears. But I capped them off. It was that same wellspring of emotion that had instigated this journey.

Settling back, I blinked and let the steady heat from the fire warm me. Katharine returned carrying a tray. The steaming pot of tea took center stage, wearing a chintzquilted dressing gown, gathered at the top.

Even the china teapots are treated to coziness here.

"I've warmed two scones for you, and this, of course, is your clotted cream. I've given you raspberry jam, but if you would prefer strawberry, I do have some."

"No, this is fine. Perfect. Thank you."

Katharine lifted the festooned teapot and poured the steaming liquid into my waiting china cup. I felt for a moment as if I had stumbled into an odd sort of parallel world to Narnia.

As a young child I had read C. S. Lewis's Narnia tales a number of times. In the many hours alone, I had played out the fairy tales in my imagination, pretending I was Lucy, stepping through the wardrobe into an imaginary world.

Here, in the real country of Narnia's author, I considered how similar my surroundings were to Lewis's descriptions of that imaginary world. A warming fire welcomed me in from the cold. But instead of a fawn inviting me to tea, it had been a kilted clansman. Instead of Mrs. Beaver pouring a cup of cheer for me by the fire, it was a tall, unhurried woman in a red evening gown.

An unwelcome thought came and settled on me as clearly as if I had heard a whisper. *Miranda, how much longer will you believe it is "always winter and never Christmas"?*

Chapter Two

$\mathcal{J}$ ignored the mysterious whisper that had caught me off guard and quickly took a sip of the steaming tea.

"Very nice." I nodded to Katharine, who still stood near the table as if waiting for my next request.

"Did you come to Carlton Heath for Christmas?" Her voice was soothing.

"Yes. Well, no. Not for Christmas. I'm just . . . I was trying to find . . . I'm . . ."

"Just visiting?" she finished for me.

"Yes. Just visiting."

Now that I was inside the teahouse, I felt much less intimidated by the reason for my journey than I had when I stood alone outside. With my guard down, I looked up at gentle Katharine and said, "May I ask you a question?"

"Certainly."

"I was trying to find the Carlton Heath Photography Studio on Bexley Lane. I walked up and down both sides of the street as far as I could go, but I didn't find it. Do you know where it is?"

She shook her head.

"I have the name printed on the back of a photo." I lifted from my big purse the plastic sandwich bag in which I'd carefully placed the photograph. I handled it cautiously. That single photo was the precious piece of evidence that had driven me here to Carlton Heath on a whim after a very long time of indecision. Removing the wallet-sized photo from the clear bag, I turned the picture over, pointing to the name stamped on the paper: "Carlton Photography Studio, Bexley Lane, Carlton Heath." I handed the photo to Katharine carefully.

She looked mystified. "This is the only Bexley Lane in Carlton Heath. I don't know of any photography studios along the road. Perhaps they went out of business."

"That's what I was afraid of."

As she tilted her head, her silver earrings caught the light from the fire. "If they were in business here, I'm sure someone around town would know about them. I've only lived in Carlton Heath for a few years, so I'm not too helpful when it comes to the comings and goings of the past. My husband would know."

She paused before turning over the photo and asked, "Would you mind if I had a look at the picture?"

"No. Please do. And tell me if you recognize either of the people in the photo. I was hoping someone at the photo studio might have an idea who they were."

The image she gazed at was ingrained in my memory. I had stared at the photo so long in my adolescent years that every detail of the two people was familiar, including the nasty, faded green shade of the sweater the little boy was wearing. He appeared to be four or maybe five years old and was seated precariously on the lap of a man who was dressed in an odd-looking Santa suit. The boy was wailing, mouth open wide, head tipped back. His short arms were rigid at his side as if he was being a brave little soldier about the situation, but he wasn't too afraid to let his voice be heard.

I knew every line in the face of the man who was playing Santa Claus. His outfit resembled a Bohemian-style dressing robe rather than the usual red velvet Santa suit. Nor was his red cap typical Santa attire. Instead, it rose to a point before tipping to the side, and it was trimmed sparingly in black piping rather than the customary wide band of white fleece.

The whiteness in the photo was found in the man's long, flowing beard and in his thick eyebrows. He seemed to be trying to keep a straight face, yet his eyes merrily revealed his mirth as well as his age. The exposed laugh lines around his clear blue eyes put him past fifty, by my estimation. His large left hand, visible around the boy's middle, displayed a gold ring on the third finger and the edge of a gold watchband around his wrist.

"What a charmer," Katharine said as she looked at the photo. A smile grew on her lips.

I nodded. The photo couldn't help but bring a smile to any viewer.

"Curious," she said, tilting her head. "I believe I've seen this picture before."

My heart rose to meet the sip of hot tea I had just swallowed. I put the cup back in the saucer, not completely on target, and kept my eyes fixed on Katharine. "You have? Here in Carlton Heath? Do you remember where?"

"No. I'm not sure. I do remember the photo was in a frame, though. An ornate frame. It was lovely. I can't quite remember where I saw it."

I waited eagerly as she stared again at the photo and pursed her lips.

After a full minute she said, "I have a suggestion."

"Yes?"

"I'm not able to place where I've seen this photo, but someone in town might know. Others who have lived here longer than I have would also know about the photography studio. One of them might possibly recognize the man or the boy in the photo, as well."

"Whom should I ask?"

"Several residents, actually. My husband, for one. He and the others will be at the performance this evening. Why don't you come with me?"

"The performance?" I repeated.

"Yes, the Dickens play, *A Christmas Carol.* I should warn you, though, it's a rather wry version. But the resident thespians have kept up the tradition for more than forty years. Mind you, the play is an abbreviation of the original, and the adaptation of the characters is, shall we say, loose. But it is wonderfully entertaining."

I bit my lower lip and felt a sickening knot tighten in my stomach.

"Would you like to come, then?" Katharine asked. "As my guest, of course."

"I . . . I don't know."

"Ah." She handed back the photograph. "Perhaps you have plans. It is Christmas Eve, after all."

"No. I mean, yes. I do have plans. I need to get back to London. To my hotel room."

"Che-che-che. London is close enough. You won't have difficulty returning later in the evening."

I scrambled for an appropriate response while Katharine stood tall and graciously patient before me, hands folded across the front of her lovely evening dress, waiting for my reply.

"I don't have the right kind of outfit with me for the theater," I said.

She smiled. "I don't think anyone in attendance tonight would even lovingly refer to what you'll see as 'theater.' What you're wearing now is entirely appropriate. I'm dressed as I am because I've a part in the production. In the concessions, actually."

I stalled, looking down at the untouched scones on the china plate.

"Well, then," she said, easing my silence. "Perhaps I'll leave you to enjoy your tea, and you can take a moment to consider the invitation. If I can bring you anything, do ask."

As she turned to leave, I unexpectedly blurted out the reason for my indecision. "I don't go to plays."

Katharine's expression appeared unaffected by my strange declaration.

I added a little more information. "I stopped going to plays a long time ago and . . ."

The resolve that had fueled my boycott when I was nine years old now waned in the light of this room where all my logic and defenses seemed unnecessary considering my hostess's elegant grace.

". . . I don't go to plays," I finished lamely.

She stood still, a few feet away. After a pause, she spoke.

"What I have always loved about decisions is that you can make a new one whenever you like."

Then she slid behind the curtain that cordoned off the kitchen area from the half a dozen open tables covered in their crimson cloths and dotted with flickering votives. I sat alone by the comforting fire.

Yet I didn't feel entirely alone. A select convoy of early childhood memories gathered in the empty seat across from me. They rose to their full height, leaned closer, and stared at me, waiting to hear whether they still held power over my decisions.

Chapter Three

$\mathcal{I}$n the silence and safety of the Tea Cosy, the echo of my gloriously odd childhood bounced off the sooty hearth and returned to me.

All the memories began with my mother. She was an *actress*. Not an actor. Please. An *actress*. She introduced herself as "Eve Carson, the actress," and people responded with a hazy nod of vague familiarity. The truth was, none of them had ever heard of her.

Each summer Eve Carson, the actress, cavorted about the stage, embodying some immortal character or other at the Shakespearean theater in Ashland, Oregon. The rest of the year she packed our forest green Samsonite suitcases into the hatch-back of our little blue car, and we traveled up and down the West Coast, calling on her string of theatrical connections.

In Santa Cruz, my mother went to work wearing a Renaissance costume that was sewn by a bald woman who had seven cats and no television. In San Diego, our hotel room was right next to the dinner theater where my mother sang and danced every night in a sailor suit. Performances were twice on Saturdays, and the food was plentiful, if I didn't mind eating at midnight, which, of course, I didn't.

I was a gypsy child. An only child. As such, I believed every-thing my mother said, including her embellished account of how, one moonlit night, she slept beside a lake on a feathery bed of moss.

"Silently, so silently, the Big Dipper tipped just enough to drop one small yet very twinkling star into the hollow of my belly. That tiny star sprouted and grew like a watermelon until . . ."

Her deep, midnight blue eyes would widen as she declared that one day, without warning, I popped right out and peace-fully went to sleep in her arms.

"And that day, my darling," she would conclude in her win-some voice, as a plumpness rose in her high cheekbones, "was the happiest day of my life. You became to me the sun, the moon, the stars, and all my deepest dreams fulfilled. Never doubt the gifting of your being or the beauty of your light, my sweet Miranda."

Like a baby bird, I swallowed every juicy word that tumbled from my beautiful mother's mouth. We looked alike, with our dark hair, defined eyebrows, and slender legs. Her eyes were the deepest shade of blue before the color could be called black. My eyes, however, were the fairest shade of blue with the sort of transparency seen in a marble when held up to the sun. The lightness in my eyes and skin transferred to the feathery light-ness of my logic, as well.

Until I was almost nine, I had no formed sense of reason. I was a child with delayed rational development. I didn't under-stand the peril of such an existence with such a woman. I didn't know a fine line existed between art and deceit. I couldn't tell when she was performing and when she was telling the truth. All of it was real to me. Every word, every smile, every tear.

My strongest memories begin with the day we drove into Ashland. The hillsides of southern Oregon were paling from green to yellow, and the hot scent of the drying grass came through the car window like a faint sweetness riding over the sticky smell of the eternal 5 Freeway's tar and asphalt.

We checked into our room at the Swan Motel on a Tuesday afternoon and ate pizza, sitting cross-legged on our bed. After that, we were living in the rhythm of her performance schedule. Every day seemed to be a Wednesday or a Thursday. It didn't matter. My mother only came back to our room to sleep for a few hours during the darkest part of the night.

Most days I would go with her to the theater, where I would find new ways to make myself invisible. For a nine-year-old I was fairly successful at my career as a phantom. When I wasn't so successful, the next day I always had a babysitter named Carlita, who brought me cookies made with pink coconut.

A few times I stayed by myself in the motel with the door bolted and the television turned up as loud as it would go. I never told anyone that my mother left me alone.

The best mornings were the ones when I would wake to the sound of water running in the shower. That meant she wasn't going to sleep for hours while I tried to stay quiet. On those mornings I would stay in bed, pretending to be asleep, and soon my mother would lean close with her long, black hair dripping tiny kisses on my face. She would say, "Awaken, my little bird! Let us fly away and dine on golden sunbeams."

Those were the mornings we crossed the street holding

hands and ate breakfast at the small café with the purple flowers by the front door. We always sat next to each other, nice and close, in the red vinyl booth. I always ordered waffles. Waffles with strawberries that came cold and mushy and tasting of freezer burn. Over the waffles and strawberries I would hold up the small jug of maple syrup and pour a spinning circle of liquid gold. The first touch of golden syrup on my tongue tasted like joy.

Eve Carson, the actress, always ordered scrambled eggs, with tomatoes instead of hash browns, and a small grapefruit juice. As the waitress walked away, I would watch my mother slip six or eight packets of sugar into her purse. She nabbed them in one smooth motion without taking her deeper-than-the-Pacific blue eyes off of me. One time she took a spoon. My mother was very good at the small things.

Whenever we were cozied up to each other like that, I didn't feel neglected or jealous of the hours she spent doting on her other love, the theater. When I felt her close, I found it easy to believe that I was to her the sun and moon and stars. I believed everything she said.

Until the day I found the blue velvet purse with the golden tassels.

Chapter Four

efore I found the purse, I found the one-eyed
dragon.

If I had believed in an ordered universe at that time, I would
have understood why the one came before the other. But as I
mentioned before, I was young in my logic and naive in all areas
of theology.

The discoveries came close to each other while we lived in
Ashland. On a beastly night during the second month of our
stay at the Swan Motel, our air conditioner stopped working.
It was too late to ask the front desk to call a repairman. And it
was too hot to sleep.

My mother told me to lie still and imagine I was a snowflake, floating on an iceberg in Alaska. I tried, but it didn't work.
My Method acting skills were sadly lacking.

"Then come with me, my little fish," she said. "We shall go
for a swim."

"Now?"

"Yes, now."

I followed my mother down the stairs, both of us in our
thin, cotton pajamas. The motel pool was small and separated
from the parking lot by a chain-link fence lined with sheets

of hard green plastic. All the outside lights of the Swan Motel glowed with a pale weariness as if they were too hot to shine their brightest and had turned themselves to dim.

"It's still hot out here," I whispered.

"Yes, it is," she murmured in the stillness. "Hot as dragons' breath."

My mother lifted the latch on the gate that led into the pool area. She walked right in as if the "Pool Closed After 9 PM" sign applied to everyone but us.

"They'll be looking for a cool watering hole this night." She dipped her foot into the shallow end. "When they come, you will allow the dragons to drink as much as they like, undisturbed, won't you?"

I nodded.

"Your movements in the water must produce only the tiniest of ripples."

I nodded again and lowered my thin legs into the water.

That's when I saw him. The one-eyed dragon.

In the darkness of the still waters, the smoldering light under the diving board appeared to be the half-opened yellow eye of a camouflaged dragon gazing back at us.

A shiver raced up my torso.

Ignoring the dragon, my mother demurely slipped her slender frame all the way under the water, submerging with barely a sound. I watched as her oversized pajama top billowed around her like a jellyfish.

Bravely lowering myself into the water only up to my neck, I kept a watchful eye on the dragon in the deep end of the pool.

He did not move. Neither did I.

The gap between us remained a flat distance of undisturbed, watery space.

My mother swam about freely, silently. I bobbed and blinked only when I had to. Then she motioned for me to follow as she slipped out of the pool.

We trotted as quickly as we could back to our room.

With a finger to her lips, she said, "We must hurry before one of them follows us into our room. Dragons are drawn in by the scent of chlorine."

She silently slid the key into the door and jiggled it once, twice, three times.

"Hurry!" my tiny voice begged. The legs of my cotton pajamas clung to me as the dripping pool water puddled at our doorstep, leaving more traceable chlorine with every drop.

"Open!" my mother commanded the doorknob. Suddenly the key worked. We pressed through together as I stifled my squeals.

My mother quickly shut the door, locked it, bolted it with the chain, and motioned for me to cautiously peek out the front window behind the closed curtain. I squinted at the submerged yellow eye that hadn't moved from the pool's deep end. We stood together, barely breathing in the darkness, reeking of chlorine. My heart raced deliciously.

A few days later I was in our motel room alone, waiting for Carlita to arrive. I had planted myself in a chair beside the window and was watching a girl in a flowered bathing suit as she squealed and splashed in the pool.

I wasn't on a vacation like she was. I lived there at the Swan Motel, and I knew all about the yellow-eyed dragon that came out on sweltering nights and breathed his fiery breath across the pool water. I wondered if I should tell her.

The blithe girl scrambled up on her father's shoulders, plugged her nose, and did a clumsy free-fall dive into the deep end. She did it again. And again. She had no fear.

I wanted to do that. I wanted to gallop down to the pool and join them. I wanted to be the next one to dive off the shoulders of the laughing girl's strong father into the pool. I wanted what she had.

Hurrying to put on my bathing suit, I returned to the chair by the window. As soon as Carlita arrived, I would convince her to take me down to the pool. I would finagle my way into the father-daughter diving contest somehow. Once I did, I would be the best diver of all. The girl's father would cheer the loudest for me.

Then something inside me said no. That would never be so.

The man in the pool was her father. He was not my father. He would always cheer the loudest for her. No father would ever cheer the loudest for me.

That was the first time I realized what a gift a father was. And I hadn't been given such a gift.

Carlita came puffing up the motel steps and bustled into the room, wheezing with apologies for her delay.

"I want a father," I said.

Carlita chuckled. "Most girls your age want a pony."

"Well, I don't want a pony. I want a father." I stood up and put my hands on my hips, imitating my mother's extended chin gesture just so Carlita would know I wasn't making a childish request.

"You have a father." She set down her small bag of groceries.

"I do not."

"Yes, you do. Everyone has a father. Every person who has ever been born has a father. A father and a mother. It takes the two for you to be born."

I scowled at her. Carlita had no magic in her words the way my mother did.

In a more instructive tone she said, "This does not mean that every child gets to live with both her father and her mother. But you do have both. Everyone has both. You have a father, Miranda."

"Then where is he?" My voice was still defiant but diminished.

"Your father is somewhere. I don't know. Maybe he is dead. It does not matter. You have a mother who loves you and cares enough for you. You should be grateful. Now sit down. I have brought you some cookies."

That night, when my mother slid into bed next to me, I pretended to be asleep. When she was making the soft, sighing sounds of sleep, I rolled over and whispered to her, "Do I have a father?"

"Hmmm?"

I had often heard her carry on conversations in her sleep. Sometimes the half sentences were lines from one of her performances. Other times she twisted her neck and yelled at people with a muffled fierceness I never heard in her waking hours. My plan was to make her respond to me while those mesmerizing eyes of hers were shut.

I wanted to know the truth, so I tried to sound like an adult. "Eve Carson, the actress, does your daughter, Miranda, have a father?"

What proceeded to roll off my mother's naked lips was

the familiar litany of the moonlight and the moss and me, the watermelon that popped out.

Her answer was acceptable to me. Under careful examination she hadn't changed her story. Clearly, I didn't have a father. Carlita was wrong. She didn't know everything the way my mother did, and I would tell Carlita that the next time she came.

But Carlita didn't come the next time.

Instead, her teenage daughter, Angela, came. When Angela arrived, I had discovered a splinter in the palm of my hand, but all the pinching and biting I tried did nothing to bring it to the surface. Angela made me go look for a sewing kit so she could use the needle to remove the splinter.

"Your mother must have a little sewing kit somewhere," she prodded. "Every mother does. Look in all the drawers."

I dutifully scoured our sparse belongings and made a discovery. The bottom lining of my mother's green Samsonite suitcase was loose. It could be removed. Under the flat panel I saw for the first time the blue velvet purse with the golden tassels.

"Is that a sewing kit?" Angela asked.

"I don't know."

"Well, open it!"

I lifted the top flap of the purse. The smooth fabric was folded over like an envelope. I carefully shook the contents onto the bed. The inventory included a folded-up playbill of a production of Shakespeare's *The Tempest* with my mother's name next to the character "Miranda." Also inside was a certificate with a raised emblem in the corner and a wallet-sized photograph of a wailing young boy in an awful green sweater sitting on the lap of a bemused, wizard-looking Santa Claus.

Without a blink, Angela picked up the paper with the raised emblem. She took one look at it and repeated the same truth her mother had told me. The truth that my own mother had successfully kept hidden from me.

I did indeed have a father.

I had a birth certificate that came from a hospital, and even I knew that papers with raised seals on them had to tell the truth. The paper had a name written in on the line above the word "Father." The name was Jay Ames. He was real, my father. And my mother had kept him from me.

That day I vowed I would never go to another play. It was the only way I could think of to get back at Eve Carson, the actress, for all her lies, all her grand performances, all her many worlds of make-believe.

I denounced fables and fairy tales. Every mythical creature she had ever introduced me to ceased to exist. The tooth fairy, the Easter bunny, and especially Santa Claus.

The only fable I still believed in was the yellow-eyed dragon that drank from our motel pool on scorching nights. I had *seen* him.

In place of my imaginary friends, I secretly began to believe in my father. I believed he must be somewhere on this earth, lying in wait, with one eye open, wondering about me the way I wondered about him.

Chapter Five

"More tea?"

The question from Katharine reached into the depths where I had gone in my memories and carried me back up to the present and to England and to this place of comfort and serenity.

"I've brought some hot water." Katharine placed a white ceramic teapot on the table. "I can bring fresh tea, if you like. If you wish only to warm up the pot you have, you can add the hot water. The tea leaves might have made the tea too strong by now."

"Okay. Thank you."

She didn't step away.

"The scones are very good, by the way."

"Would you like another?"

"No. I will take the bill, though. How much do I owe you?"

"Nothing." She waved her hand. "Let this be my small Christmas gift to you."

"No, really, I would like to pay." I reached for my wallet.

"Not this time," she said with a calm firmness. "This time I would like to give to you. Next time you can give to me."

It seemed strange that her hospitality-clad services alluded to a "next time." I thought I had made it clear that I was passing through and had no plans to stay or to return.

"Have you decided then about the performance this evening?"

I paused. All my self-preservation instincts told me to be on my way. Ignore the possibility that someone else in town might be able to identify the man and the boy in the photograph. I didn't need to know. The mystery of my father's identity could die with me the way it had died with my mother eighteen years ago. If my mother were here today, she would be thrilled to go to the performance. I was not.

"Would your mother like to come, then?" Katharine asked.

I looked at her hard. Had I said something aloud about my mother? I thought my reminiscences had been only in my mind.

Several friends and roommates had told me over the years that I talked in my sleep as well as in my waking. They told me when I was deep in thought I would carry out the process half in silence and half in mutterings. I must have mentioned my mother, thus prompting Katharine's question about her.

"My mother passed away quite some time ago."

Surprisingly, I felt secure enough to add my simple, well-rehearsed paragraph. It was a disclosure that evoked sympathy while at the same time closing the door on the topic.

"She fell from a scaffold at an outdoor theater in Salinas when I was eleven. It was a dress rehearsal for *The Merchant of Venice*. She died from internal injuries two days later. However, the show did go on."

I realized that what I had just revealed to Katharine sufficiently explained why I wasn't on speaking terms with the theater. Even without my boycott of all things make-believe, this information was enough. Katharine certainly would withdraw her invitation to the Dickens performance.

She seemed unruffled, though. "I'm quite sad for your loss."

I nodded my appreciation for the care in her voice. Now that we had that piece out of the way, as often happened in my relationships, I felt we could go on to the business at hand. My business, as I saw it, was to be on my way to the train station.

Katharine's business seemed to be waiting for an answer about the play.

"I need to go back to London." I pushed the chair away from the table and slung my big purse over my shoulder. "Thank you again for the tea and the scones. They were delicious." I paused at the front door. "Are you sure I can't pay you, though?"

"Next time," she said with a smile. A silver earring peeking out from under her dark hair caught the light of the candle on the table and gave me a silvery goodbye twinkle.

I stepped out into the cold with much less gusto than the kilt-clad "Christmas Present" had earlier. Immediately, the chill went through me, and I wished for a longer coat.

"That's what I'll give myself for Christmas," I said as I headed downhill on Bexley Lane.

This time I knew I was expressing my thoughts aloud. It didn't matter. No one was around to hear me. I decided I would spend tomorrow, Christmas Day, in my London hotel room. Understandably, I felt most nostalgically at home whenever I was in a hotel room.

Then the day after Christmas I would go out shopping for a new coat. Surely London had after-Christmas sales that rivaled the ones in San Francisco.

That way, when I returned to the office next week, I would have something to show for my on-a-whim spree to London.

My legs stretched to their full length as I picked up my pace and retraced the path to the train station. Windows on either side of the lane were lined with festive decorations that jived in the gale that accompanied me, whistling down the lane. One of the two-story brick buildings was adorned with a single lit candle on each windowsill of the four symmetrical windows. Another place of residence had a large pot by the front door in which a four-feet-tall evergreen was strung with twinkling white lights and red bows tied to the ends of the branches.

I turned the corner toward the train station and pulled the collar of my peacoat closer to my ears. The charm of the Tea Cosy pervaded the village of Carlton Heath. If I ever decided to believe in fairy tales again, this would be the setting in my mind's eye.

Long, slender branches on the tall trees spread their protective embrace over glowing streetlights and stone cottages. The trees didn't seem to notice that they had lost all their foliage. Their role hadn't changed with the fierceness of the seasons; they still sheltered the people and the dwelling places on Bexley Lane.

I kept walking. Down the hill, around the corner, and past the ivy-covered chapel. I paused only a moment to have a look at the softly lit church with the arched entryway. It seemed to me as if the church were wearing her rambling cemetery like an appliquéd blanket. The blanket tumbled from the foot of the rose bed and fell haphazardly over a hundred sleeping kernels of life, lives that had built the chapel, paved the roads, and taken tea beside many a soot-covered hearth.

Now they were all silent.

One life. That's all we get. When will mine be silenced? Or should I be asking when will it truly begin?

I crossed the street and tried not to think of anything but my numb feet all the way to the train station. The station had a covered platform and a little station house. A single bench rested against the waiting area's back wall. A newspaper kiosk was positioned in one corner, and the ticket booth filled the opposite corner next to the blinking cash machine.

Aside from the ATM, everything else about the room I sat in to be away from the cold looked and felt as if it hadn't changed in fifty years. I noticed one modern addition. An electronic sign was positioned over the door listing the trains' times and destinations in a trailing news flash. To the right of the contemporary timetable was an old-fashioned, round-faced clock. I consulted the clock and then the sign with the trailing, red-dotted letters. The next train to London was scheduled to leave in twenty minutes.

My watch still gave the time as 11:58. I tapped it again and held it up to my ear. No sign of life could be heard.

Maybe I'll buy myself a coat and *a new watch for Christmas. Or at least a new battery.*

I sighed and leaned back. I was the sole traveler at the station. The only other person in the building was a dozing gentleman who sat on a stool, manning the newspaper kiosk.

Glancing again at the wall clock I wondered, *What time is it in San Francisco?*

Not that it mattered. I didn't have anyone back in the City by the Bay waiting for me to call him or her. No one would wonder why I wasn't coming to dinner on Christmas Day. I had covered all the bases at the office. I was a holiday nonentity.

That thought wasn't a comforting one. I could leave the country—or this planet, for that matter—and very few people would realize I was gone.

How did my life come to this?

Apparently the career I had begun at such an early age as a backstage apparition was still in effect. I was invisible.

Discontentment over my invisibility had fueled my passion-fire last week when I decided to book a ticket to London. I had been lying alone in bed, wide awake in the middle of the night, when I concluded that I had lingered too long at the shallow end of my life, staring across the divide at the unblinking father I had chosen to believe in. If he did exist, I needed to know. If for some reason he wasn't ready, willing, or able to come to me, then I would make the first move. I would float toward him and see what happened.

Hence, here I was in England. And nothing had happened.

"Well, I tried," I muttered defensively. I had followed the few clues and had tracked down the village of Carlton Heath only to find that the photography studio no longer existed. What more could I do?

There was Katharine's statement that she thought she recognized the photo. Someone in Carlton Heath quite possibly had a copy of the same photo I had. Someone who might know something.

Could I really leave now and have no regrets? Would I be content returning to San Francisco with nothing more than a new coat or other after-Christmas-sale merchandise? What about the answers I had come in search of?

No one else knew the purpose of my trip. But I knew. And I knew that a week from now, when I lay awake in the middle of the night, I would ask myself why I had given up so easily. Especially when one small lead still dangled in front of me.

I thought of what Katharine said about decisions.

You can make a new one whenever you like.

For several long minutes I didn't move. I thought briefly— only briefly—about what it would be like for the kernel of my short life to be tucked under a blanket of cold earth. Could I die knowing I had not exhausted all possible leads to finding my father?

Rising and pressing back my shoulders, I stepped away from the waiting room bench, drew in a deep breath, and made a new decision. I decided to go to the theater.

"Merry Christmas, Mother," I muttered. "I am going to see a play."

Chapter Six

$\mathcal{G}$rey Hall, where the Dickens performance was being held, was easy enough to find. I had roused the dozing clerk at the newspaper kiosk inside the station, and he had given me clear directions in the most charming accent I had heard yet during my nearly seven hours on English soil.

The walk from the train station was uphill, and the temperature had dropped another few degrees. At least the wind had died down. The exertion of heading uphill warmed me as I walked. The distance was farther than I had estimated, and I hesitated at the second crossroad.

It's not too late to go back to the train station. You don't have to do this.

"Yes I do."

The abiding thought that kept me walking was that I needed to know. I needed to know who my father was, and I needed to know him. The only clues I had to his existence had led me to Carlton Heath. Although I didn't understand my trailing thought, I sensed that as much as I needed to know, I also needed to be known.

One determined foot in front of the other brought me into Brumpton Square and there, set a short distance off the main road, stood the Victorian-style meeting hall. Eight metal shepherd's hooks lined the walkway, and from each hook hung a lantern, illuminating the path in the crystalline air. Ropes of evergreen garlands draped the entrance, and magnificent curls of gingerbread façade on the building's face disguised its true age. The name, Grey Hall, appeared across the front of the theater in raised letters.

A large dedication plaque beside the entrance read, "Dedicated May 19, 1987, The Society of Grey Hall Community Theatre." The building had been constructed over a century too late for a Dickens appearance, yet it felt easy to believe that the author himself might be in attendance this evening where past and present seemed to have merged.

No other theatergoers were in view as I stood in front of the closed doors. My guess was that I had missed the opening curtain. I reached for the long handles on the double doors and slowly opened the right side just enough to slip into the foyer.

A short woman in a flowing pink evening dress came to my side. With a gloved finger held to her lips, she motioned for me to follow her to the far left of the reception area where a thick, blue velvet curtain separated us from the theater seating.

The woman's short, tousled hair was as pink as her dress and dotted with sparkles. Her perfectly shaped lips were painted the same cotton candy shade and dotted with a jewel above her top lip on the right side, a distinguishing beauty mark. She appeared to be in her early forties; yet, dressed up as she was, her heart seemed much younger.

Without a word, she drew back the curtain and nodded for me to step inside the dark arena. I entered and stood to the side, waiting for my eyes to adjust.

A booming voice called out, "Come in, come in!"

It was the merry Scotsman. For a moment I froze, thinking he was extending the invitation to me.

In actuality he was delivering the line onstage to a very short Scrooge who stood trembling before the ominous presence of the kilted greeter. Behind the Scotsman was an open door.

The invitation was repeated by the man with the wide, wooly-white sideburns. "Come in, come in, and know me better, friend!"

"Who are you and what is this place?" Scrooge cried in a pipsqueak voice. Under a long nightshirt and floppy cap, the leading actor was obviously a child.

My spirit softened to all things theatrical. Some images of make-believe had never truly left me, no matter how belligerent I had been about them. Just as I had earlier remembered wanting to be Lucy walking through the wardrobe into Narnia, I now found myself disarmed by this classic Dickens character, who brought an Oliver Twist feel to the role of the miserly Scrooge. I could see myself in the pint-sized presence who now held center stage.

The Scotsman wore a trim jacket atop his kilt and finished the look with a flat sort of hat perched slightly to the side and sporting a feather. From under the hat flowed a cascade of wavy white hair. I'd seen his balding head uncovered at the tea cottage and knew the tresses were part of his costume, but the tumble of hair was convincing.

Taking his cue, the Scotsman declared, "I am the Spirit of Christmas Present."

I smiled. *So he really was a Christmas Present, just as he said.*

"What will you do to me, Oh Spirit of Christmas Present?" Young Scrooge asked.

"Enter, and you shall see." Christmas Present stepped to the side, and the sliding prop door was moved off-center by unseen stagehands. Where a dark closure had been, a wonderful spread of Christmas cheer was revealed, with a flickering fireplace, a tree trimmed in lights, a stack of gifts, and a table spread with a feast.

"All has been made ready for you," the Spirit of Christmas Present declared. "Come."

Scrooge hesitated.

In that moment, I felt my defenses slide off me like pool water. All had been made ready for Scrooge, and yet he hesitated. I saw how I had been in that same Bah Humbug role for many years. I understood the hesitation. The standing back and not trusting. But no one had ever made a celebration ready for me and invited me to come in.

An old fountain of tears I had kept capped for ages began to leak. Instead of looking for a seat in the back of the hall where I could watch the rest of the play anonymously, I slid through the velvet curtains and returned to the reception area.

Feeling around in my large shoulder bag for a tissue, I didn't notice the woman in pink as she came to my side.

"Here," she whispered. She held out to me a handkerchief with a pink rosebud embroidered in the corner. Once I'd dried my eyes and curbed my tears, I held onto the handkerchief and stared at the crumpled cotton in my hands as the woman patted my arm.

I told her in a mumble that it had been a long day, hoping

that would explain my breakdown. But I wasn't sure I could even explain to myself why the image of a feast and gifts accompanied by a warm invitation to Scrooge had struck such a chord of longing inside me. I sensed that Young Scrooge was being offered everything I wanted but didn't know how to find.

Taking a deep breath and summoning another round of fortitude, I whispered that I was fine. Really.

With a nod of understanding, she continued with the gentle pats on my arm. All the while she seemed to be trying to fix her gaze on my eyes. Even in the dimmed lobby lights, I was sure the weariness of jet lag showed. No doubt she was checking for more tears. I had successfully repressed them and my eyelids were now puffing up with the reserves. Dabbing my nose, I continued to look away. She continued trying to look me in the eye.

"Well, thank you." I awkwardly held out the used handkerchief. I wasn't sure if I should offer to have it laundered before returning it. I had never been given a handkerchief before.

"Keep it," she said softly.

I hadn't decided if I was ready to go back for the rest of the performance. But she made the decision for me by ushering me through the velvet curtain and pointing to an empty chair in the second row from the back. I had just enough time to settle in and refocus before Scrooge began to argue with the Spirit of Christmas Present over his discomfort at the revelations he had faced during his waking dream.

With his skinny arm dramatically shading his gaze, Scrooge cried out, "Take me from this place, I beg of you, oh, Spirit of Christmas Present. Do not force me to look any longer at what I have become. Tell me instead what is to come."

"And so it shall be." The Spirit of Christmas Present turned, and his kilt's pleats kicked up. Scrooge stood alone on the stage. The lights dimmed as Scrooge drew both fists to his mouth, frightened as a mouse.

"Please! I beg of you! Do not leave me like this!"

All the lights extinguished, and silence covered us all. Then a shuffling of feet and clicking of theater seats rolled across the room as the curtain closed and the lights came up slowly.

While the rest of the audience rose and made their way to the lobby for intermission, I stayed in my seat, taking in my surroundings. The auditorium was smaller and narrower than I had pictured in the dark when I entered. Fresh boughs of evergreen had been shaped into huge Christmas wreaths that hung from Victorian-style lighting sconces. The ceiling was inlaid with plaster frescos that had a repeating pattern of mellow golden white on purer white. The padded seats were covered in deep blue velvet and matched the dark blue velvet of the stage curtains that were trimmed across the top with golden tassels.

The deep blues reminded me of my mother's eyes. She would have liked this theater. She liked small, intimate settings where she felt she could wrap her arms around the audience and keep it in her embrace.

I settled into the comfortable seat and took in the whole "envelope"—the size and shape of the theater and the deep blue velvet stage curtains with the golden tassels. In a strange way, I felt as if I were sitting inside an enlarged version of my mother's secret blue silk purse. Now I had become one of the curious clues hidden under the tasseled flap.

he blue velvet purse had been given to me along with the rest of my mother's meager possessions after her death. She had no other surprises in her green Samsonite suitcase nor in any previously unrevealed secret places such as a safe-deposit box. She left this earth without providing a clue as to how to find another living relative such as a grandparent or aunt.

In light of my true orphan status, Doralee, the bald woman in Santa Cruz with the seven cats and no television, gathered me up.

When I first went to live with Doralee, she was determined to track down my father and do the right thing—give him the option of claiming me. All we had to go on was the name listed on my birth certificate, Jay Ames.

Doralee checked all the "Ameses" she could find. Nothing matched up. After weeks of diligent searching, we came to the conclusion that, true to form, my mother had invented my father's name on the birth certificate.

I then became Doralee's "niece." My new aunt proved to be as skilled as my mother had been at fabricating information to fit comfortably into what people wanted to hear. Documents were created as needed to enroll me in public school for the first time in my life. Stories of my genealogical history were embellished to satisfy probing principals, and Doralee made sure that I was well clothed with her own sewing-machine creations.

Whenever I started to sink into myself, she would do this funny little wiggle of a dance and sing, "Everybody doesn't like something, but nobody doesn't like Doralee." I trusted myself to her.

One day at school a girl I didn't like was singing Doralee's song.

"Where did you hear that?" I demanded.

The girl and her friends stared at me as if I were a freak, which in some ways I'm sure I must have been, even in Santa Cruz. They all sang the song together and then told me it came from a commercial for frozen pastries on TV.

I had never heard the commercial because we didn't have a TV, and we never, ever ate frozen pastries. We ate only organic foods and socialized with an eclectic group of all-natural free thinkers. Birthdays and holidays weren't celebrated, but journeys to enlightenment were encouraged with gatherings and music and dance.

I told those three girls to "buzz off," only I used a more earthy term than that. Afterward I never belonged to anyone or any group the rest of my time in school.

Four years into our make-believe family affair, Doralee's cancer returned, and two things happened. Actually, three.

The first pivotal event was Doralee's reading a book that prompted her to spurn all her earthy rituals, burn down a shrine in the backyard, and embrace an oddly traditional form of Christianity. She prayed regularly in the name of Jesus Christ and read entire chapters of the Bible every day.

"The true return to Eden is found in Christ," she told all her friends. "Not in this lifetime, in these fallen and broken bodies. It's all yet to come, in eternity. Everything we've longed for can and will be fulfilled in Christ. He is coming back to claim all that is rightfully his, including the souls of all who have been adopted into his kingdom."

Doralee lost a lot of friends, especially toward the end, when her passion for God, heaven, and her new, resurrected body were the only things she wanted to talk about. Even up to the hour of her passing, she didn't waver from her claim that she had received a new life—an eternal life—when she trusted in Christ. She kept talking about "the Lamb" redeeming her.

I was with her that afternoon. I watched death come and take her, and it was astonishingly beautiful. Her expression transformed from the constant pinch of agonizing pain to a smoothness and a very real absence of fear. Her aura was the closest thing I had ever seen to genuine peace. And then, as I watched, she left her body.

The second significant event with Doralee was that, before her pain became unbearable, she revived the search for my father. She made a list of all the names of actors who appeared on the playbill of *The Tempest* and set about trying to track down any one of them. The dates of the performances listed on the playbill were nine months before my birth date. Doralee made the connection one day and concluded that one of the participants in the theatrical company might know something or someone. Or one of the actors might be someone. Someone such as my father.

Fifteen years is a long time when it comes to picking up a trail on a troop of gypsies. None of the leads went anywhere. However, Doralee's realization that the performance dates of *The Tempest* connected to my birth played on me for years.

The third turning point occurred after Doralee's death. As an unusually savvy fifteen-year-old, I chose to emulate the lifestyle of deceit that had been so professionally demonstrated to me over the years. I left school, and since I looked older than I was, I fabricated the few necessary documents to appear eighteen. Then I moved to San Francisco.

Within a week I had effortlessly landed a job as a waitress at a large hotel and had enrolled in a bookkeeping class. I wanted a career in numbers and not words because even I knew that numbers couldn't lie.

For the next thirteen years I remained steadily employed at an accounting firm in the Transcontinental Building. I had a nice studio loft with an excellent view of the Bay Bridge, a loosely held circle of friends, no cats, and two ex-boyfriends. Josh, the longest running boyfriend, was the one who had unknowingly prompted me to make my journey to England.

I should have realized why a graduate psych student who wanted to work with abused children was keenly interested in me. Josh was convinced I was hiding something.

My clear-eyed response to him had been, "I had a wonderfully unusual mother, and she was very protective of me. I was not abused."

Josh went with my answer but always seemed to be looking for more. "Not all abuse is physical," he claimed.

I had become such an expert at making my history invisible that the only details I willingly handed over to Josh were airy and unsatisfying to someone who wanted to one day make his living analyzing the human psyche.

Up until Josh, everyone who sincerely asked about my life before San Francisco was given the sparse yet dramatically satisfying account of how my mother had died in the arms of her other love, the stage. Orphaned, I'd gone to live with an "aunt" who later died of cancer. If the interviewer probed further, I easily sidetracked him with details about Doralee's seven cats, all named after Egyptian pharaohs.

Josh was the only person, aside from Doralee, who didn't stop probing about my father.

Early in our relationship I told Josh, "My father is dead. He died before I was born."

Then one night, in an uncharacteristic blip of vulnerability, I showed Josh the blue velvet purse. I showed him the playbill for *The Tempest* and the photograph. I did not show him my birth certificate. He thought I was twenty-seven. This wasn't the time to reveal that I was twenty-four.

Josh took the photograph and held it like a forensics expert would. "What if your father is alive, and these two clues are your trail to find him?"

I shrugged. All I had experienced in the past were dead ends.

"The photo looks old enough that this screaming boy could possibly be your father."

"Maybe."

"One thing we know is that the man in the photo is dressed as Father Christmas. There's no doubt. He's a British version of St. Nick, if I ever saw one."

Josh studied the stamped wording on the back of the photo. "The Carlton Photography Studio must be located in England then. Or somewhere in the UK. It shouldn't be too difficult to track down a lead on 'Carlton Heath.' It could be a town or a family name. And then you've got Bexley Lane, which is going to narrow it down for you. You have some key pieces here."

Josh speculated that my father might still be in the UK, but I told him my mother had never been abroad. At least she never had told me about being out of the US. If my father was from England, how and where did my mother meet him?

Josh didn't yet have a theory for that piece of the puzzle. He turned the photo over and over, deep in contemplation. Looking up at me with a lightbulb-over-the-head expression, he said, "It's a wallet-sized photo."

"Right." That fact was obvious.

"What if this picture was kept in a wallet?"

Now I was getting impatient with Josh, the amateur analyst.

"Don't you see? Your mother had a relationship with this man, and when she realized the relationship couldn't last, she stole what she could—a photo. She took it from his wallet."

Josh had no idea how close he was getting to the truth of how my mother would operate. I alone knew how smooth my mother could be at performing such a sleight of hand. But when? Where?

I took the photo back from Josh and noticed for the first

time how pointy Josh's ears were. He wore his hair too short for a person with such ears. On that night of my vulnerability, I stared far too long at his ears.

Two weeks later I used his ears as a frivolous excuse when a girlfriend at work asked why I broke up with Josh. "It's because of his ears," I told her. "I looked at him one night and realized I could never stay in a serious relationship with a man with such pointed ears."

She stared at me in amused disbelief.

"Think about it. If we had children, they would all come out looking like elves!"

A week later she asked Josh out to coffee on the premise of consoling him over our breakup. I think the two of them are still together. I'm glad. Josh deserved someone sincere. I had not yet learned how to fully develop that quality. But to my credit, I was trying.

I will always be grateful to Josh for his analysis of my mother's treasured pieces of evidence. It took me several years to move forward with Josh's leads and to allow myself to believe my father might be findable. Once I tracked down the village of Carlton Heath, a half-hour train ride southeast of London, it only took a few more clicks on the computer to find Bexley Lane.

And here I was.

I glanced around the auditorium and thought of Josh. He would have been happy to know I had taken this risk. He also would have been surprised that I set foot inside a performance hall.

The theater lights flickered the universal cue for the audience to return to their seats. I stood to let a trail of people pass me. Settling back, I gazed around the theater and realized I was sitting in the presence of my former competition—my mother's old love, the theater.

The lights dimmed. With a sigh, I nodded my acceptance.

Merry Christmas, Eve Carson, the actress. This is my gift to you. It's the only gift you ever asked of me. The gift I resisted giving you for so many years. Tonight I have made peace with your beloved theater.

Chapter Eight

*J*ust before the curtain went up, I involuntarily glanced at my watch. The hands had moved one minute, now reading 11:59. Odd. I liked it when numbers were dependable. Having a broken watch was getting to me.

Wee Scrooge in his flapping nightshirt rose from the center of the stage on a belt and pulley and flew out of his bed crying, "Oh, Spirit of Christmas Present, speak kindness to me that I might not faint from lack of hope."

Offstage the Scotsman's booming voice replied, "You have yet a few more images to view before this night is passed."

I smiled at the sight of flailing Scrooge being whisked back and forth across the stage on the sophisticated rigging. One of his slippers fell off, prompting a ruffle of chuckles from the audience. The Peter Pan touch was endearing.

Just then I felt a soft tap on my shoulder. Katharine stood in the aisle, motioning for me to follow her out into the lobby. I slipped out as quietly as I could.

"I see you came," she said. "I'm glad. What do you think of our liberal adaptation?"

"It's clever. The young actor playing Scrooge is doing a great job."

"Yes, he is. Listen, I won't keep you from the last half. I wanted to speak with you before you left. Ellie was the one who told me you were here."

I remembered the rosebud-embroidered handkerchief in my pocket. "Is Ellie the Sugarplum Fairy?"

Katharine chuckled softly. "Yes, and she'll appreciate that you recognized her costume. I'm afraid I asked if she had come as a pink snowflake."

"I heard that." Ellie moved across the lobby to join us.

"I was just about to extend the invitation to the cast party at your home."

"Yes, do join us. We would be delighted." Ellie stepped up with a metal cash box in her arms. "I have to run this out to the car. Katharine, you and Andrew would be able to fit one more guest in your car, wouldn't you? Oh, and I'm Ellie, by the way."

"I'm Miranda."

"Miranda, you will come, won't you?"

Katharine added, "It would be the simplest way for you to connect with someone who might know about the photo. All the insiders from around Carlton Heath will be at the party. Please say you'll come."

I hesitated, concerned about catching a train back to London afterward.

Katharine and Ellie assured me I could find a ride to the train station whenever I was ready to leave the party. They both appeared eager for me to join them, so I took a small risk and said yes.

I returned to my seat, settled in, and enjoyed the entertainment. The local actors seemed to be giving the performance their all. Tiny Tim closed the night with one final "God bless us, everyone!" and the applause rose as the curtain fell. Cheers, chuckles, and more applause continued until the entire cast appeared onstage for a bow. I had forgotten how radiant some actors were when they stepped out of their characters and stood under the shower of streaming applause.

Those were the times my mother glowed.

Katharine was waiting for me in the lobby. She and her husband, Andrew the Scotsman, offered me a ride to Ellie's home.

We climbed into their compact car and were barely out of the parking area when Andrew said, "Did my wife tell you we've been married fourteen months come this Saturday?" He was still wearing the hat with the flowing white hair and was driving on what my brain kept thinking of as the "wrong" side of the road. I was seated in the front, at Katharine's insistence. The place I occupied should have been the side fitted with the steering wheel and brake pedal, were this an American car.

"And what about you? Are you married then, Miranda?" Andrew looked at me, but I wished he would look instead at the dark and narrow road we were rolling down at a precarious speed.

We seemed to be heading out of town. For a moment I wondered why I had entrusted myself to these strangers. At home I would never blithely jump into a car with people I had just met. Nor would I go to any sort of party held at the home of people I didn't know.

A voice in my heart was telling me what I hadn't expected to hear on this trip. This journey was changing me. Change had not been my goal.

"Are you then?" Andrew asked, looking at me expectantly.

"I'm sorry. What did you just ask?"

"I asked if you're married?"

"No, I'm not."

Andrew looked over his shoulder at Katherine. "Are you thinking what I'm thinking?"

Katharine didn't answer, but I nearly did. I was thinking: *You'd better keep your eyes on the road!*

Andrew glanced forward and then back at me. "I'm thinking you should meet my son, Ian. Will you be staying over the Christmas holidays?"

"Yes. I mean, no. Not here in Carlton Heath. I'm staying in London."

"Are you now? Have you got family in London, then?"

"No. I—"

"Andrew, my love," Katharine interrupted, "you've missed the entrance."

"Awk! I have indeed." With a quick turn, he set the small car in the opposite direction and steered through an open-gated entry to a large home lit up with tiny white lights around the eaves.

The home wasn't a manor per se. Not that I had ever been to a manor to compare it with Ellie's home. But it was grand, distinct, and impressive.

The large two-story house, composed of dull red brick, was dressed up with a grand arched entrance, tall rounded windows, and a fairy-tale-like turret in the south corner. Nothing about the picturesque structure looked standard or mass-produced. It seemed like a one-of-a-kind creation sprung from an artistic mind. The closer we drove, the more beautiful each curve of the house appeared in the headlights of Andrew's car.

"What a beautiful place," I said, wishing I could find better words to describe how the house made me feel.

"The house was built by Edward's grandfather, wasn't it, Andrew? Or was it his great-grandfather?"

"It was his great-great-grandfather. He was an artist of some fame. Have you heard of the Pre-Raphaelite Brotherhood, Miranda?"

I shook my head.

"Aye, well then, I don't imagine it would much matter to you who the builder was or why it was built in such a fashion, nor why Edward is so keen to keep the place as it is."

"And who is Edward?" I asked, lost in the conversation.

"Edward Whitcombe. Ellie's husband. Son of Sir James Whitcombe." He looked at me as if waiting for a response. "Have you not heard that name before? Sir James Whitcombe?"

I nodded slightly. I thought I had heard the name, but I wasn't sure where.

"We consider Edward and Ellie Whitcombe our resident touch of royalty, I suppose."

"Royalty?"

"Are you stretching the matter a bit, Andrew?"

Andrew cut the car engine and ignored his wife's admonition. "You see, when Edward's father was knighted by Her Majesty a number of years ago, it gave a certain rise to the village status. Katharine and Ellie have been friends for a long stretch. That's how Katharine came to settle here in Carlton Heath, not long after the passing of her first husband."

"Andrew, I'm not sure all of this family history is going to be useful to Miranda."

"Right. Well, to finish what I had to say about Edward and Ellie, I call them our resident Lord and Lady, just to get a rise out of them. They're nearly like family to us, wouldn't you say, Katharine?" Andrew slid out of the car and held out his hand to help Katharine disembark.

"Yes. Almost like family to us." Katharine slid her hand through Andrew's arm. He offered his other arm to me, and I played along with being escorted by Christmas Present across the gravel driveway. A dozen other cars were parked in the expansive area between Andrew's car and the house. We could hear sounds of laughter from inside as we traipsed through the cold air up to the well-lit front door.

Pausing under the arched entry, Andrew knocked soundly on the massive oak door. I noticed a banner of words painted over the doorway in a Victorian script: "Grace and Peace Reside Here."

The door swung open, and Lady Sugarplum Fairy welcomed us with her rendition of Andrew's line from the performance: "Come in, come in, and know me better, friends!"

"Well, there you have it," said Andrew. "Next year you're the one to play the role of Christmas Present, Lady Ellie. You have the lines already."

"Lovely! I was thinking an all-female cast would be a clever twist next year. What do you girls think?" Ellie's hair swished as she turned her head to look at Katharine and me. The motion invited a shower of pixie dust to leave her pink hair and rest in sparkles on the threshold.

"Do come in out of the cold before you answer that," she added.

"The answer is simple." Andrew motioned with a half bow for Katharine and me to enter first. "Have we not caused the poor man enough reason to turn over in his grave each Christmas when we take such liberties with his story?"

"Undoubtedly," Katharine stated.

Andrew removed his hat, hair and all, and handed it to our hostess as she collected our coats. "Then I propose we try something radical next year. We perform the blessed script the way it was written originally!"

"Bravo!" Ellie laughed. "Wouldn't that take the town by surprise!" Looking at me she added, "I'm so glad you've come, Miranda."

"Thanks for letting me crash your party."

Ellie looked at Katharine as if she wasn't sure why I would say such a thing.

"You're not crashing into anything. It was my idea for you to come. Katharine tells me you have a mystery to solve. I'm eager to hear about that, but first I must put away these coats. Katharine? Andrew? You will pick up my duties as hostess, won't you? Please make sure Miranda meets all the right sorts of people."

Ellie whooshed away in her pink gown, and I had a feeling my peacoat would forever carry sugarplum sparkles on it.

Ellie added a final thought over her shoulder. "And do avoid introducing her to the seedy characters, won't you?"

"Not a chance," Andrew said. "We're taking her directly to all the questionable guests to give her a true impression of the sort of individuals you associate with."

"That would include you, Andrew," Ellie called as she exited down a hallway.

With a wink and an aside to me, he added, "The only person I want to introduce you to is my son, but he's not here. So how about if I let Katharine carry on the introductions? If either of you needs me, you know where you can find me."

I glanced at Katharine, and she interpreted. "He'll be wherever the food and drinks are. Come. I suppose we should start with an introduction to our host, Edward. Do you have the photo with you? Perhaps you might show it to him."

I realized I had blindly handed my coat and purse over to Ellie. "No, I left it in my purse. Which way did Ellie go?"

Katharine pointed down the hall to the left. "She's probably put all the coats in the study. It's the second door on the left. Would you like me to go with you?"

"No, I'll be right back." A small and probably childish part of me wanted to roam about the poetic home by myself. In front of me was a polished staircase just begging to be climbed the way an unattended piano on an empty stage begs to be played.

I reluctantly turned from the stairs and went down the left hall of the L-shaped floor plan. The second door on the left led into a large study with built-in bookshelves on either side. In the air lingered a hint of worn leather and cherry almond pipe tobacco. In the center of the room sat a great desk made of a dark wood that had been polished until it reflected the amber light of the standing floor lamp.

Wow. One could rule a small country in a room like this and with a desk like that.

I spotted my coat, hanging from a standing coatrack near

the door. My purse shared the same hanger. As I lifted off the purse, I noticed the collection of photographs on the wall. All the pictures were framed in black. The center one caught my eye, and I stepped closer. Her Majesty, Queen Elizabeth, was standing beside a well-dressed man, whom I guessed to be Sir James Whitcombe. His stately appearance and perfectly groomed dark hair gave him a sophisticated air of royalty.

The framed photo directly under the knighting of Sir James was a contrasting image of the debonair figure. He was stretched out on a picnic blanket, eyes closed, as if trying to take a summer nap. Over him stood a little girl with ringlet curls and a mischievous grin. She was dropping rose petals on his face one by one.

I cast a sweeping glance over the other three pictures. One of them showed an informal family gathering around an outdoor table. Another was of Sir James and a lovely blond woman, whom I supposed to be his wife. The two of them stood with their arms around each other in front of the Taj Mahal. The third photograph was of Sir James sitting atop a camel with a hazy view of the great pyramids of Egypt in the background.

Leaving the study with my purse, I told myself to be on my best behavior. I had never been in such a home before nor in the company of people who possessed such wealth.

I realized I should have felt nervous or at least a little uncomfortable about being around all these people I didn't know. Strangely, I felt calm. Welcomed. Warmed. Ready to welcome Christmas Present with this glad company.

Chapter Nine

The largest room in the Whitcombes' luxurious home was referred to as the drawing room. When Katharine and I entered, I stopped and tried to take in the architectural features as well as the gorgeous decorations. Ellie had made use of her sugarplum theme by incorporating pink touches throughout the elegant room. Swags of greenery looped around the room at ceiling level. Tiny white lights and clumps of holly berries were woven into the garlands, which also were dotted with pink sugarplums.

The ceilings were high, and the voices of the thirty or so lively guests echoed in the large open area. Even though the room provided enough space for everyone to be comfortably seated, most of the visitors were standing, chatting in small groups. At the far end of the room a bushy Christmas tree was lit up with pink lights. At the other end, closer to the door where Katharine and I stood, was a long table covered with a smorgasbord of food.

"Be sure to try the crab puffs." Katharine handed me a china plate. "Ellie serves them with a fabulous sweet-and-sour dipping sauce."

I made my way down the line, filling my plate with

petite appetizers of all shapes and adding a spoonful of each scrumptious-looking salad. We stood as we ate, balancing our plates and being careful not to bump into anyone or spill our cuisine.

Katharine introduced me to a stout woman who had lived in Carlton Heath her entire life.

"Miranda is curious about a photography studio on Bexley Lane," Katharine said. "Do you know anything about the Carlton Studio?"

"Well, yes, of course. Wonderful people, the Halversons, weren't they? They were in business there on Bexley Lane for years. Such a pity when they moved, wasn't it? We had our family photos taken at their studio when the children were young. Such a loss when they went out of business, don't you think? One can only assume the failure of the enterprise was the result of the computer industry. All the digital cameras for sale these days. People are too impatient to wait and have something done right or to go to a specialist to have it done. They would rather take care of everything themselves at home on their computers. I don't have a computer. I don't plan to get a computer. This is all leading to terrible destruction, really. Don't you think? I tried to get my grandson to go one entire day without using any of his computer gadgets, and do you know, he would not do it. He would not. It's not only the computers, is it? It's all the other machines they carry with them to listen to their music and make all their unnecessary phone calls. Quite irritating, really. Have you seen them on the trains these days? All wired up as if they belonged in a hospital bed in the cardiac ward. They have this wire that goes to this ear and this wire that goes to that ear. Somehow they talk through something and carry on conversations that are entirely too private while out in public. It's deplorable, really."

As the stout woman paused for air, I glanced at Katharine, and she attempted a polite escape for us. "Yes, deplorable. If you don't mind, I've a few others to introduce Miranda to before she slips out to catch the train to London."

"You'd best check the schedule for the times. This being Christmas Eve, you know. I'm sure you've considered that. Tomorrow, of course, being Christmas Day, well, it goes without saying that when it comes to National Rail, I'm of the opinion that it, such as it is, is not accommodating the travelers trying to be with family for the day. No, I would think it's more along the lines of National Rail trying to accommodate all the employees who would doubtless ask for outlandish additional wages on the holidays. Not that anyone—"

Katharine interjected, "Oh, I see someone I need to introduce Miranda to. You will excuse us, won't you?"

Before the woman could answer, Katharine nudged me across the room through the maze of people. Some of them were still in costume, which made the gathering a familiar setting and awoke childhood feelings in my heart. Doralee had a lot of opinionated friends like the woman we had just listened to. I was much more comfortable around that sort of party guest than the ones who might ask me questions. It was all part of my preference to blend into the background when in a crowd.

We came through the human obstacle course with our plates of food intact and only a few bumps. A tall, dark-haired man stood in front of us, holding in one hand a small plate emptied of appetizers and in the other hand a piece of fluted stemware with some sort of pink beverage.

He wore rectangular-shaped glasses that gave him an English professor aura in a cool retro sort of way. He looked like the young teacher-of-the-year sort of professor who could be living on a sailboat near Belize if he chose to but instead spent his days shaping impressionable minds with the classics.

The person with whom he was chatting had just stepped away, making a natural opening for Katharine to move closer and make the introductions.

"Edward, I would like you to meet someone. Miranda, this is our host, Edward Whitcombe."

"Son of Sir James Whitcombe," I added, without realizing I was drawing from my earlier conversation with Andrew in the car.

Edward tilted his head with a vague weariness. "Were you a fan, then?"

"A fan?"

"Of my father. Were you a fan of his work?"

I glanced out of the corner of my eye at Katharine, hoping for some sort of clue as to what Sir James did or why I should be a fan. But she had turned to greet another guest, leaving me alone with my bumbling mess.

"I . . . I don't know."

Edward looked oddly humored by my response. "I believe that's the first time I've heard that answer."

I looked down at the uneaten crab puff on my plate and considered popping the whole thing in my mouth so I would be assured of not speaking for at least thirty seconds.

Instead, I chose an unusual path for me, especially with strangers. I spoke the truth. Rather involuntarily, I might add.

"I'm from the US and . . ." If my lack of British party manners hadn't already given away that I was an outsider, I was sure my American accent had. I tried another approach. "What I meant to say is that I'm not familiar with your father or his work. So I don't know if I'm a fan or not."

"Is that right?"

I nodded. "I am familiar with his name only because of a few details Andrew and Katharine told me as we drove over here tonight."

"And they didn't tell you what my father did?"

I shook my head and offered a tiny smile, hoping my faux pas would be dismissed.

He nodded slowly. It was the kind of nodding motion one makes when thinking. He kept looking at my eyes the same way his wife, Ellie, had tried to make eye contact with me at the theater.

I realized how jet-lagged I was and how much I could use a little freshening up before I tried to carry on a serious conversation with anyone else in the room. At least if I wanted them to take me seriously. I reminded myself that my objective was to see if any of these guests had a lead for me on the photograph.

For a fleeting second I considered asking Edward if I might show him the photo and ask for his input. But I felt off balance and didn't want to risk offending the "Founder of the Feast" by letting him know the only reason I was there was to carry out some amateurish detective work.

Instead of continuing the conversation in any direction, normal or abnormal, I looked away from his questioning gaze. "Would it be all right if I used your restroom?"

"Our restroom? Do you intend to have a rest?"

"Excuse me?"

"Were you asking if you might lie down to take a nap?"

"No. I would like to use the restroom . . . the bathroom . . . I want to wash up."

"Oh, of course. The WC. It's in the hallway, to the right of the stairs."

"The what?"

"WC. Short for water closet, of course."

"Oh. Thank you." I turned to go, wondering how it could be that though we were both speaking English, neither of us understood the other.

"Aren't you going to ask me what my father did?" he asked.

I stopped and looked at him over my shoulder. I wasn't sure of the proper way to respond, so I simply took the cue as if it were a riddle. "What did your father do?"

With a hint of grin he said, "My father was a famous actor."

Without a feather of a thought, I said what came immediately to my mind, borne of my life experience. "Then I'm very sorry for you."

A smile burst onto his face. He gave me an appreciative nod and raised his nearly empty glass in a toast.

I tried to inconspicuously slide out of the room.

Chapter Ten

I gave myself a stern lecture in the bathroom mirror. Or the "WC" mirror. Or was it a "looking glass" like in *Alice in Wonderland?*

Whatever it was I was looking into and whatever tiny room I was in with the itty-bitty sink and pull-chain toilet, I gazed at my pale expression and reminded my sorry self that I had never been particularly good in social settings and that this evening was further proof.

"Try to be polite, Miranda. Get some information, and then get out of here. Don't make these people remember you for all the wrong reasons."

Taking a minute to comb back my dark hair, I gathered my shoulder-length mane up in a clip and found some lip gloss for my dry lips in the side pocket of my shoulder bag.

Slightly freshened, I returned to the drawing room. The guests had gathered in an organized circle, and a game of some sort had begun. I stood at the back, observing. It took me only a moment to realize what type of game had been initiated. This was a company of actors and other theater aficionados. They were playing a form of charades, of course.

The guest who stood in the center of the room recited a line from a play, and everyone else tried to come up with either the play's name or the line that followed.

I hung back as a large man took to the center of the room and called out, "'What light through yonder window breaks?'"

The group laughed at his attempted falsetto.

Young Scrooge was the quickest to shout out, *"Romeo and Juliet!"*

Hearty pats on the back were in order for nimble Scrooge, who then moved to the center and recited one of his lines from the performance that evening.

"'Do not force me to look any longer at what I have become. Tell me instead what is to come.'"

The immediate response came from Andrew, as he delivered the following line in his Spirit of Christmas Present stage voice: "'And so it shall be!' That would be from *A Christmas Carol*, of course."

The group rumbled with comments on how, from then on, the lines should be from plays other than *A Christmas Carol*, especially because the Carlton Heath adaptation had so mercilessly slaughtered the original lines, making the quotes less than authentic. Everyone gave Scrooge a kind word or two, saying he'd done just fine.

Andrew moved right along with, "'Does it occur to you, Higgins, that the girl has some feelings?'"

"My Fair Lady," someone called out.

"Also known as . . ." Andrew prompted the group, as if this were a trick question. To add to the clues, he continued with the next line, "'Oh no, I don't think so. Not any feelings that we need bother about. Have you, Eliza?'"

"'I got my feelings same as anyone else,'" I said, filling in the next line under my breath. Only one person heard me. That person was Ellie.

"Well done, Miranda! You should receive extra points for coming up with the next line." To the group she said, "The play is *My Fair Lady.* Why are you stalling, Andrew?"

"Ah!" Edward stepped forward and said with a triumphant flash, "*My Fair Lady,* originally entitled *Pygmalion.*"

A collective "of course" sigh rippled across the room.

"Miranda, were you in a performance of *My Fair Lady* at one time?" Ellie asked.

"No, I've never been in a play."

"Really? Neither have I. I like you better by the moment. Here I thought I was the only one in this group who was inexperienced on the stage."

I didn't respond to her comment because I couldn't say I was inexperienced on the stage. I just had never officially been in a performance. My mother had played the role of Eliza Doolittle on a stage somewhere when I was around six. She taught me how to read with that script.

Edward was in the circle now. He paused, thinking, glancing around the room. He looked at Ellie, as if seeking some bolstering of his courage. She glittered and glowed and blew her dashing husband a kiss. The charming moment led me to believe that Edward was much more humble than his circumstances would have suggested. I felt a fondness for both of them, which surprised me because I barely knew them.

Edward kept looking at Ellie, and then his sweeping gaze turned to me. In that moment, he seemed to have found his line.

I told myself I could be imagining the connection, but when I heard his line, I knew I had inadvertently inspired him. It was my name. He delivered Miranda's final line in *The Tempest*:

"'O wonder! How many goodly creatures are there here! How beauteous mankind is! O brave new world that has such people in't!'"

No one in the room responded. They looked at each other with shrugs and mumbles.

"Where did he come up with that one?" Ellie shook her head at her husband and showered my arm with her fairy dust.

"It's from *The Tempest*," I said, being sure to keep my voice low.

"*The Tempest*?" she asked. "Shakespeare, right? How do you know all these lines?"

I shrugged, hoping to appear naive. I hadn't seen a production of *The Tempest*. I knew the line because I had read the script many times. During my years with the television-less Doralee, I read. I didn't go to plays, but I read dozens of them, many times over.

Edward repeated his line with an eyebrow partly raised in anticipation of victory at the parlor game. "Anyone? Anyone at all? Even a guess?"

I felt fairly certain it wasn't polite to one-up a host. Ellie didn't seem to think the same way.

"She knows it," Ellie said, pointing at me. "Go ahead, Miranda."

All eyes turned toward me.

I froze and then realized the best way to get all eyes off me was to say the answer. "*The Tempest*."

Edward looked impressed, or maybe the better way to

describe his reaction was "intrigued." He bowed and made a sweep of his hand to show that the floor was mine. I had forgotten about that part of the game. It was my turn to stump the experts. I didn't want to be in the center of this group.

"That's okay." I raised my hand and stepped back, closer to the fireplace. "You can go again. I don't have any ideas. Just, please, go again."

"But it's your turn," Ellie said.

"Really, I can't . . . I don't have . . ."

My expression must have reflected my discomfort because Ellie, the perfect pink hostess, stepped forward. "Miranda gave her turn to me. And I have a good one. Are you ready?"

I appreciated Ellie more in that moment than she could ever know.

To avoid further embarrassment, I backed up a few feet from the rest of the group and stood beside the leather chairs by the hearth.

Ellie dove in with a line I didn't recognize. Another woman knew the play, shouted the answer, and gleefully took the spotlight.

I noticed Katharine across the room and remembered why I had been invited to this party in the first place. Glancing around for a clock to see what time it was, I wondered when I needed to leave for the train station. I spotted an antique clock tucked in among the decorations on the mantel. Taking two steps closer to the fire to see the correct time on the small face, my eye caught a lineup of family photos in an assortment of frames. In the first photo, a little girl stood beside an elaborately decorated Christmas tree. She wore a frilly dress with a wide sash around the middle and shiny black Mary Janes with white, cuffed ankle socks. She stood up straight, sporting a great big cheesy smile. Her arms were so closely pressed to her sides that her very full skirt was flat on either side while swooping out in the front and back like a canoe with a ruffly petticoat.

Next to that sweet picture was a larger photo. This one was of a little boy wearing pajamas and a pair of brown felt reindeer antlers. His expression was pure eight-year-old glee as he peered inside the partially unwrapped Christmas gift on his lap.

Moving on to the most ornate frame next to the clock, I drew closer, and my breath caught in the back of my throat.

It was the picture. *The* photograph. Father Christmas and the wailing boy. The exact photo I was carrying in my purse, only the picture on the mantel was larger and less faded. And in an ornate frame, just as Katharine had said she remembered. The picture was here. In this home.

I sank into the leather chair beside the fire and felt the room fold in on me.

How can this be? Who are these people?

The truth I had been seeking all these years was so close I could touch it. Only I couldn't move. I could barely breathe.

Chapter Eleven

y thoughts scurried around, trying to form some sort of order.

Who is the man in the photo? Who is the boy? What is the photo doing in this house? Why did my mother have a copy of that picture? Was Josh right? Did my mother know one of the people in the photo? Is one of them possibly . . . my father?

The game was beginning to wind down. Ellie floated through the circle of guests, urging them to have more food. I leaned forward, hoping to catch her eye. My unspoken request worked, and she came toward me.

"Would you like something to drink, Miranda?"

"No, I . . ."

"Have you tried the sugarplum punch yet? It's not spiked. At least I don't think it is. Trouble is, I haven't managed to keep my eye on Andrew all evening so I can't guarantee he hasn't instigated his usual shenanigans. Would you like something else to eat?"

"No, I . . ." I glanced at the mantel, feeling my heart pressing against my chest with firm thumps. "I . . . I wondered . . . is that . . ."

Ellie looked at the clock on the mantel. "Are you looking for the correct time? Because if you are, that clock is notoriously slow. You need to leave here in time to catch the train back to London, isn't that right?"

"Yes, but . . ." I instinctively glanced at my watch. Regardless of the actual time, the hands had moved another minute. They were now pointed straight up. Midnight. My journey through Christmas past and Christmas present had brought me here, to this "midnight moment." The photo in my purse matched the photo on the mantel; the past, present, and future had intersected.

"You would have no trouble catching the 10:42 to London, if you left here in about ten minutes," Ellie said. "Or fifteen, if you like. I would be happy to give you a ride to the station. How does that sound to you?"

I couldn't leave yet. Not until I knew . . .

"Ellie, I . . . I . . . The photo on the mantel. Who are those people?"

"Our children. They were downstairs at the beginning of the party, but they have both gone off to bed. Perhaps you didn't see them. That's our daughter, Julia. She's five now. And our son, Mark, is twelve."

"And the other photo? The one by the clock?"

"Isn't that the best? I love that picture! Everyone loves that photo. Everyone but my husband. I had to fight with Edward to put it out this year. His mother always had the picture there on the mantel at Christmas. You would think after more than thirty-five years my husband would give in to displaying it every year. Doesn't it capture a four-year-old's tantrum perfectly?"

"So that's Edward? The boy in the photo is your husband?"

Ellie nodded, smiling fondly at the photo.

I estimated Edward and Ellie to be in their late thirties or early forties. Edward wasn't old enough to be my father. That meant . . .

"The man in the photo?" I ventured, rising to my feet and standing next to Ellie for a closer look.

Ellie looked surprised that I didn't know. "That's James, of course."

My ears seemed to have opened to hear what Doralee and I had missed all those years ago. "Jay Ames," I repeated.

"That's right, Sir James. Edward's father."

I felt my legs wobble and lowered myself back into the leather chair.

"Sir James played the perfect Father Christmas for years. I remember sitting on his lap when I was five and having my picture taken. He gave me two lollies for being such a good girl that year. I really thought he was *the* Father Christmas."

"Sir James Whitcombe," I repeated, feeling the weight of his name on my tongue. Sweeping the room with my gaze I asked, "Is he here?"

Ellie looked at me oddly. "Do you mean, is he still alive?"

I nodded only once, not sure I could bear the answer either way.

"No. He passed away a year ago September. Perhaps the news wasn't as publicized in the US. I can tell you this: he was a wonderful man, regardless of what you may have read in the rags. He deserved to be knighted as he was. The lies that were said about him over the years were terrible. Just terrible. Sir James had so much dignity, so much integrity, that he never fought against the slander. He let people have their say and never went up against them to prove them wrong. I remember one time after Edward and I were first married when . . ."

Another wellspring of long-suppressed tears bubbled over my lower lids.

"Oh, you poor dear. You must be exhausted, and here I am, blathering on." Ellie perched on the side of the chair and patted my arm. "Katharine said you only arrived today. I'll get your coat, and we can be on our way to the station now, if you like."

With another pat on my arm, she added, "You know, it's such a pity you're not staying on in Carlton Heath. We do have a guest room, if I could at all persuade you to stay. We would be delighted to have you join us for Christmas dinner."

Before I could process the idea of staying, Andrew strode into the center of our conversation. "You've done it then, Miranda, haven't you?"

"Pardon?"

"The snow."

"Snow?" Ellie repeated.

"Have you not looked out the window since we arrived?" With a nod toward me Andrew said, "I asked if you had brought the snowflakes with you, did I not? What I should have asked was how much snow you planned to be leaving with us."

A number of the guests gathered by the front window, peering out into the twinkle-lit darkness. Several already were leaving the party, and the headlights of their cars spotlighted the slanting flurry of snowflakes.

Two of the older guests stepped up to Ellie, saying they had decided to be on their way before the roads became disagreeable. She hurried off to gather their coats and mine, promising to be right back.

I tried to think. It had all come at me so quickly.

What should I do? Should I show Ellie and Edward the photo? Then what would I tell them? That I have reason to believe Sir James might be— no, could be—my father?

"I can't do that," I mumbled.

"Can't do what? Stay on for the night? Of course you can." Andrew was still standing close by with a glass in his large hand. "I heard the invitation with my own ears. If you stay on, there's a good chance I can introduce you to my son."

Finding an easy smile for the endearing man in the midst of all my pulsing thoughts, I realized what an idyllic setting this was. I couldn't, I wouldn't, toss a grenade into the middle of this lovely family on Christmas Eve. I needed to leave. I didn't belong here. I needed time to think.

"Andrew," I said plainly, "I need to go back to London. I know Ellie offered to give me a ride to the train station, but do you think I might be able to ride with you and Katharine instead? I need to leave right away."

"Are you sure you want to be leaving?"

"Yes. If you don't mind."

Andrew tilted his head and slowly began to wag a finger. "You know what it is? It's the eyes. That's what it is."

He looked at the photo of Sir James on the mantel and back at me.

"Aye, that's what it is. It's the eyes. Like a mountain stream in the highlands, that's what they are. You have the clearest blue eyes I've seen since Sir James, rest his soul."

I swallowed and looked away.

"Now, he was a man of honor, he was. Why, we wouldn't be having the Dickens performances if it weren't for Sir James and his generosity to the town and to the preservation of the theater. He was a man of great benevolence. I like to think he would have enjoyed our humble show this year."

With a nod, he turned to his wife, who had joined us in the middle of his speech. I didn't look directly at Katharine. I didn't know how much of Andrew's oration she was taking in, and I also didn't know how strong her powers of deduction were. She was the only person to whom I had shown the photo. And she was standing only a few feet from the mantel. It would be too easy for Katharine to connect the dots.

"Miranda is in need of a ride. To the train station. I offered our services, Katharine. Are you ready to be on our way?"

Katharine hesitated before asking in her firm, gentle voice, "Did you find what you were looking for when you came here, Miranda?"

I paused before answering carefully with one word. "Possibly."

Katharine stood with her hands folded in front of her elegant red evening gown, and I knew that she knew. I can't explain how I knew, but I did.

I ventured a glance in her direction. Katharine was looking at me with the sort of smile that is shared between two women when one is holding the other woman's secret as carefully as a bird's egg that has fallen from its nest. It was easy to believe she wouldn't drop the precious bundle. At least not here. Not on Christmas Eve.

Chapter Twelve

$\mathcal{E}$llie strode across the drawing room toward us with my coat over her arm. Pink sparkles danced in her wake.

"I'm so sorry, Miranda. I got sidetracked. We should be on our way, don't you think?"

Before I could answer, Andrew said, "We'll be cartin' her off, so you won't have to drive in the snow." He stepped closer to Ellie and gave her a good look up and down, as if he had just noticed her outfit.

Turning to Katharine, he said, "You may need to drive, my love."

"Why is that, Andrew?"

"I avoided overdoing it on the punch, and yet I do believe I'm beginning to see pink Ellie-funts."

His pun took only a moment to sink in. As soon as it did, a chorus of groans followed.

"I will remember that one, Andrew MacGregor." Ellie held out my coat.

Andrew intercepted and held the coat for me so I might slip my arms in more easily.

"Ian will be disappointed." Andrew's boldness took over. "He would've wanted to meet you, Miranda. And what a pity you won't be staying through Christmas."

"Miranda, you are welcome to stay here with us, if you like," Ellie said. "Our guest room is ready. As I said before, we would be honored to have you for as long as you like. Truly."

Before I could slide my other arm into the coat, Andrew lowered it nearly to the floor. I turned to see what had happened, and he said, "You won't be needing this in the guest room, now, will you?"

A string of objections rolled off my tongue. I had already paid for a hotel room in London and my suitcase was sitting in that room, unopened, with everything I needed for an overnight stay.

Ellie quickly made mincemeat of all my objections and indicated with her expression that the decision had been made. I had the feeling that if I made another peep, I would be viewed as an annoyance and the invitation would soon be regretted.

My adrenaline must have been running low by that point because I took the path of least resistance and decided I would stay the night. I could collect my thoughts in the solitude of a guest room or a hotel room. The guest room was closer.

"All right. I will stay, if you're sure it's okay." I was, in a way, asking the question of Katharine as much as I was asking it of Ellie. My glance went to Katharine first.

She closed her eyes only a moment and gave her head a slight nod. It seemed as if she was granting me approval.

Ellie was much more effusive. "Of course it's okay. The more the merrier! Katharine already knows this about me, but I don't know if you do, Andrew. When I was a university student, I had the romantic notion of spending a semester in Portugal. I was alone in Lisbon over the holidays, and it was the worst Christmas of my life. The thought of you going to London but not meeting up with family or friends once you get there, well, I'm not one to tell you what to do. I can only say that, when I spent a Christmas by myself, it was desperately depressing. So you see, I have my own reasons for wanting you to stay."

I knew this group of kind-hearted people would be stunned to know that most of my Christmases had been spent alone. Ellie's invitation was offered from her heart, and from a frightened yet awed corner of my heart, I accepted.

"Now that we have that settled, we'll be on our way, then." Andrew said. But he and Katharine chatted a few more minutes with Ellie about joining the Whitcombes for Christmas dinner after the morning church service. All the plans were set, and the two of them made their way to the front door, along with most of the other guests.

I followed, not sure what else to do. At the door, Katharine turned and gave me a look that I interpreted to be reassurance that I had made the right decision and everything was going to be okay. I raised my hand in a good-bye wave as she followed her kilted Christmas Present out into the drifts of snow.

"The guest room is upstairs, third door on the right." Ellie explained that she would gather a few overnight items for me and leave them on the bed. She also said she and Edward would be up for a while longer because she had a few more gifts to wrap.

"Christmas services are at ten thirty. Christmas dinner will be at two o'clock."

The awkwardness that should have been present when

trying to fit a stranger into a family's holiday schedule was absent around Ellie. That grace was due, I think, to her easy-going manner. She seemed content to let the rest of the night and the holiday roll along at its own pace.

"Is there anything I can do to help clean up?" I asked.

All but two of the guests had gone, and one of them was clearing the serving table and carrying the dishes into another room. The other guest was leaning against the mantel, deep in conversation with Edward, who looked respectfully concerned about what the older man was saying.

"Whatever would make you feel the most comfortable, Miranda. That's what you should do. And just for your reference, the kitchen can be reached through the hall and to the far right."

Ellie took my coat from me once again and flitted off. I stood in the almost empty drawing room and didn't know what to do. Edward was still occupied with the man wearing a tweed jacket and a red woolen vest underneath. I should have been ready to head to the isolation of the guest room but, in that moment, helping to clean up seemed the right thing to do.

The other woman, a white-haired worker bee, gave brusque directions to me, as if I were her servant girl. I didn't mind. She seemed to have a system going. She also seemed to be the sort who lived to serve and loved to be commended for her service.

I cleared all the plates that had been left in the drawing room on end tables, chair arms, and bookshelves. The bee woman had a tray ready for me to stack all the plates and carry them to the kitchen. I followed the directions Ellie had given, out into the large entry hall, then to the far right.

The kitchen was well lit and surprisingly modern compared to everything else I had seen of the house so far. A large center island was at the hub of the kitchen. The island and all the counters were black marble. Gleaming copper pots hung above the stove. A painted clay pot in the window held a long-stemmed orchid that exploded with three exotic purple blooms. Beside the tropical flower was a nativity scene carved in wood and painted in primary colors that had faded since the set's debut.

Stepping closer to the kitchen sink that was directly under the wide window, I examined the crèche. The irregularities of the pieces made it look handmade. The cast seemed to be all there: Mary and Joseph, the shepherds with their lambs, the wise men in turbans with a long-legged camel, an angel with outstretched wings, all of the walk-on characters of the nativity faced the star of the evening, Christ. The infant lay in a manger lined with straw and was attended by a kneeling blue Madonna and a yellow-robed Joseph, who leaned on a staff.

I made the decision then that I would go to the church service in the morning with Edward, Ellie, and their children. I had never been to a Christmas church service. My gift to my mother had been setting foot inside a theater once again. My gift to Aunt Doralee would be to set foot inside a church.

At that moment, I knew I had made enough decisions and taken in enough information for one day. One very long day. I needed to find the guest room and let sleep cover me with a blanket of time and space so all the spinning orbs in my personal cosmos could realign themselves. The world I now moved about in was not the same world I had known for the past twenty-nine years. I needed to find my center of gravity.

I tiptoed up the stairs that had bid me to climb them ever since I entered the house. After eight stairs there was a landing with a padded window seat and a large lead-paned window that looked out on an expansive garden. I paused and watched the storm illuminated by the dim light coming from the windows on the lower floor. The garden was quickly being covered with snow.

Having spent most of my life on the West Coast, I knew little about snow. I did know that sometimes it comes to the earth as gently as a dove, leaving a feather-like covering of white on homes, trees, and country fence posts. Other times, snow comes blasting into a quiet village on vicious gales of wind and heaving sheets of ice at everything in its path. Such was the snowstorm—no, such was the tempest—that I watched that Christmas Eve.

Yet I was safe, tucked away in a spacious guest room in a home built by Edward Whitcombe's great-great-grandfather. A man who, quite possibly, could be my great-great-grandfather, as well.

Chapter Thirteen

The sort of crying I gave in to that night in the guest room was important crying. I wept as a woman in mourning. I mourned the absence of a father in my childhood. I mourned the loss of my mother at the onset of my teen years. I mourned the loss of Doralee at the launch of my young-adult years.

And I cried for myself. For the fragments of my life that might have been about to line up.

I cried into the plump pillows that lined the tall wooden headboard of the elevated guest bed. Like Shakespeare's Miranda, in the wake of the tempest, I watched and waited with a tenacity born of unfounded hope and idealized trust. The crisp white pillowcases caught all my tears and held them the way the sails of a ship gather wind.

My tears came without much sound. The few muffled sobs that leaked out went deep into the pillows and stayed there. Once the storm ceased, I knew that a season of my life had ended in that guest room. My breath returned to me in calm measures, and I began to think about what was to come. In that place of peace, I made a decision.

I would keep my possible connection to Sir James a secret. I would take the secret with me to the grave, as my mother had.

I also decided that as soon as I had a chance to see Katharine again and pull her aside, I would make her promise that she wouldn't reveal any of our shared speculations. She seemed the sort of woman who could keep a promise.

As I drifted into deep sleep, I thought about my reasoning for such a decision. My connection to this family wouldn't change anything. Whether or not Sir James was my father wouldn't change who I was or what I did or how I chose to live my life. The possibility—the evidence that seemed clear to me—was enough to satisfy me. What kind of disruption would my declaration make in this home where "grace" and "peace" were the sentries at the front door? I liked the thought of being noble. Keeping the speculations to myself seemed the most noble route I could take.

I awoke from a deep and dreamless sleep while it was still dark. The small clock beside the bed told me it was 7:09. Christmas morning.

To pad down the hallway to the bathroom, I needed to pull on my travel-rumpled gray pants, white T-shirt, and V-neck sweater. Inching the door open as quietly as possible, I tiptoed across the runner on the wood floor of the long hallway. Every third or fourth step the floor creaked, making it impossible to cover the distance without creating a dreadful amount of noise.

Attempting to run the water quietly, I washed my face, holding the cool cloth over my tear-swollen eyes. With a squirt of toothpaste on my finger, I gave my teeth a less-than-effective scrub. At least my hair was easy to catch up in a clip in the back. I didn't look my best, but I felt okay. Ready to meet whatever was ahead. My center of gravity was returning and that center was me, just as it had been out of necessity for the past decade and a half.

I was a few feet past the bathroom door when one of the bedroom doors along the hallway opened. Five-year-old Julia appeared wearing a pink nightgown and fuzzy, duck-shaped slippers. She looked out at me expectantly.

Her expression turned to a frown. "You're not Father Christmas."

"No," I whispered, with a finger to my lips, "I'm not Father Christmas."

"Who are you?" She didn't lower her voice on my cue.

"My name is Miranda. I'm . . ." I didn't know how to explain who I was. "I'm visiting your mother and father."

"Why do you talk like that?"

I kept whispering, hoping she would take the hint to keep her voice low as well. "I don't live here in England. I'm from America."

"Are you a film star?" She looked hopeful.

I shook my head.

"One time when I was little we had a film star who came to our house, and he stayed in that room." She pointed to the guest room where I had just come from. "He came to our house the day my grandfather went to heaven."

She looked at me more closely. With a tilt of her head she asked, "Did you know my grandfather?"

A knife went through my heart. "No," I barely whispered. "I didn't know your grandfather."

I bit the inside of my lip and then added before the tears could come, "I wish I could have met him."

She yawned a kitten-sized yawn.

Redirecting all my emotions, I said, "You should probably go back to bed. At least for a little bit."

"But I want to go downstairs to see if Father Christmas has come with the presents." Her dark eyes twinkled. "Will you go downstairs with me?"

My experience with appropriate protocol when visiting a family on Christmas Day was nil. The only point of reference I had was American movies in which eager children in pajamas bounded down the stairs at dawn and found a massive collection of wrapped gifts under the Christmas tree.

My childhood memories included gifts wrapped in playbills and scrawny trees decorated with silver tinsel. On Christmas morning, my mother and I didn't scramble to open our few gifts. Our tradition was to stay in bed and share a box of Whitman's Sampler chocolates for breakfast. Then we opened our presents.

My mother always clapped as I opened my gifts, which were usually items such as new socks that hadn't come from the thrift store like the rest of my clothes. Every year, I wrapped up the little bottles of hotel lotions and shampoos, and she never failed to act surprised and pleased. She would open the tops of the bottles and breathe in the scent as if I had given her a bottle of perfume direct from Paris. The rest of the day we watched holiday movies, and sometimes my mother took a nap.

"Will you come with me? Please?" Sleepy-eyed Julia tugged on my sleeve and looked adorable in her yellow ducky slippers.

I glanced up and down the hall and fell into a role I didn't know I could play. "All right. I'll go with you, but we must be very, very quiet. We don't want to disturb Father Christmas if he's still downstairs."

"Do you think he's still here?" Julia's eyes widened the way I'm sure my eyes must have widened whenever my mother verbally turned an unseen combination lock and opened to me a parallel world of make-believe.

"I don't know. We can go see. Your feet must make only the softest of tiptoeing sounds as we go down the stairs. Are you ready?"

Julia nodded and slipped her small hand into mine.

With tiny steps, we made our way down the hallway to the stairs. Nimble Julia made an "oh no" face at me when our weight on the second stair produced a loud creak.

From behind one of the other bedroom doors at the end of the long hallway I heard sounds as if someone else in the house was stirring. I hoped what I was doing with Julia was okay. I didn't know if I might be spoiling some family tradition with our descent to the lower level of the quiet house.

We made it to the landing where the stairs took a turn before continuing with the final eight steps that led into the grand entryway. I was prepared to start the next flight of steps when Julia stopped and let go of my hand.

She let out a little gasp and flew to the window seat. Outside, in the pale rose shade of the rising dawn, the world appeared as soft and airy as a pure white dove. The blush from the winter sun enlivened the snowy horizon with a glistening glow of otherworldly first light. One glance was not enough to take it all in.

I stood beside mesmerized Julia, and together we watched

the day come forth on white-feathered wings. With a touch of splendor, the undressed trees seemed transformed into regal maids-in-waiting, shimmering with icicle-shaped diamonds dripping from their elegant ears and slender arms.

"Is that snow?" Julia asked, whispering for the first time.

"Yes, that's snow. It's beautiful, isn't it?" I whispered back.

Julia nodded, her gaze still fixed on the unparalleled show outside the large window, where the day before a sleeping garden had stretched out brown and unnoticed.

I sat beside her on the padded window seat. With complete trust, she curled up in my lap, leaning her head against the soft inner curve of my shoulder.

Never before did I remember feeling as if another human was so completely at ease, sinking into me for companionship and comfort. I used to snuggle this way with my mother any chance I had. She didn't seem to tire of the positions I chose or the times when I needed the security of her touch. It hadn't occurred to me that I might one day provide that same source of tenderness for a young life.

Then it came to me that Julia was more than just any little girl. If Sir James was my father and Edward was my half brother, then Julia was my niece.

Drawing a breath for courage, I faced the fact that if I walked away from an exploration of my possible heritage, I would lose more than the sure knowledge of who my father was. I would lose the only half brother I would ever have, along with his Sugarplum Fairy wife. I would lose a twelve-year-old nephew I hadn't met yet. And I would lose my only niece, the adorable embodiment of sweetness, who was now cuddled up in my arms and whose soft brown hair smelled like warm maple syrup.

The price of my decisive nobility was going to be much higher than I had first estimated.

Chapter Fourteen

ather Christmas and gifts under the tree forgotten, little Julia stayed close to me in the window
seat. Together we watched two red and brown birds flit from
the icy branches of an apple tree and land in the fresh snow.
The early birds hopped across the clean white carpet, leaving
their tiny footprints to mark their trail to the snow-covered
bird feeder. With a flutter of their wings, the two birds pecked
and flicked through the snow before reaching their chilly
breakfast.

I stroked Julia's silky hair and hummed the only Christmas
carol I could remember at the moment—"Silent Night."

Julia leaned into me and released a contented sigh.

All was calm. All was bright.

The gift to me in that timeless moment on the bench seat
was a gift of understanding. I experienced in a small way the
bliss my mother must have felt when she held me in her arms. I
was her baby doll. To her credit, she did the very best she could
at loving me despite her disjointed life.

The years of blame I had assigned to my mother for choosing
to live within the fairy-tale castle of her own mind all seemed to
evaporate when I felt the unlabored breathing of small, trust-

ing Julia. How could a woman not choose to gather up a tiny version of herself and valiantly protect, nurture, and delight in such a marvel?

By my best estimations, my mother was eighteen when I was born. Maybe nineteen. If she had relatives she could have sent me to, she never hinted at it. If she considered handing me over to an adoption agency, it was only a private contemplation.

Her decision had been to keep the two of us together, and now I understood why. This. This closeness. This chance to share the moments of wonder together. My mother wanted me. That in itself was a precious gift.

That truth was the gift I received that Christmas morning. My mother wanted me. She wanted me close to her heart. And she always kept me there.

In that Christmas morning moment, with little Julia enclosed in my embrace, I looked out the frost-laced window and released Eve Carson, the actress, from all her failures toward me, her miniature self. I then thanked Eve Carson, the mother, for every right thing she did in proving how much she wanted me.

I wondered: If she had lived, and if I had asked, would she have told me who my father was? And if she did tell, would she have told me the truth? I knew I would have wanted the imaginary answers more than I would have wanted the unbendable truth. But still, I wondered. What would she have said if she knew I was here, in this home, with these people? What details of my existence would she at last reveal to me?

"What about Father Christmas?" Julia reached up and patted my face. "And the presents. We must go see the presents!"

I helped her off my lap, and we were about to tiptoe down

the remaining eight steps when I heard a door open in the hallway above us.

"We must hurry!" Julia whispered, circling back to the playful excitement of being on a secret mission. She padded down the stairs in her yellow slippers, reaching for my hand as she went.

I followed eagerly.

The grand entryway was even grander in the faint daylight. Soft rays of steady sunlight pierced through the colored glass in the two tall arched windows that rose like pillars on either side of the stairway. A bucket of morning glorious colors spilled over the wooden floor and caught a gathering of dust particles in the spotlight right in the middle of their waltz.

I stopped just a moment and held out my hand as if I could catch one of the lit-up dust particles the way I had long ago stopped to catch a raindrop in my palm on an Oregon afternoon. Julia tugged on my hand. "Come on!"

Scrambling, I followed her into the drawing room. All evidence of the party from the night before had been cleared away. In the corner, the full green Christmas tree was lit up with twinkling lights. Under the tree was a mound of fabulously wrapped gifts. Ellie had accomplished her late-night goal with panache.

"Oooh." Julia's eager expression was worthy of a picture. I wished I had a camera just then to capture the magic in her eyes. She hung back, looking without touching. Maybe she knew the family traditions. I guessed she knew she must wait for the others. Or maybe all she wanted was to have a peek at this feast for the eyes. Everything about the room was enchanting in the thin morning light. The dark wood of the fireplace along with the deep cocoa brown leather of the chairs set the tone of sophistication, but all the added touches gave the room its regal feel.

I joined Julia in taking in the elegance of this room that was dressed up for Christmas morning. In addition to Ellie's pink touches throughout the greenery swags and the strings of gold beads that hung from the chandeliers, I noticed other details that had been hidden last night when the room was brimming with guests. My eyes went to the hand-painted blue Delft tiles that lined the inside of the fireplace and to the large floor rug with the small red birds woven into it. An engaging pattern of waving green and gold vines was laced throughout the thick curtains that hung from the ceiling to the floor alongside the front window. The drapes were drawn back with golden cords, making a soft frame for the pristine view of the snow-blanketed world outside the window. All the room needed was a fire in the hearth to warm things up, and it would be as perfect a setting for a Christmas card as ever there could be.

A thought both tender and sad settled on me. This time it wasn't a thought about my mother or my father or my past. The thought was of my future. One day I wanted to be married. I wanted to have a daughter. I wanted her to know who her father was and to have a precious, close relationship with him. I wished that if I did have a daughter someday, I could bring her to this home, this room, on Christmas morning. I wanted her to have all this wonder.

The tender sadness covering my wish was that I didn't belong here. Not really. This wasn't my place or my world to dream about.

And yet I was here. Against all the odds, I was here. On Christmas Day. With family, really, even though they didn't know that. In my heart I knew this place, these people, were my people. And I didn't know who to thank for that. How had I ended up here?

The coincidences were too many. If there truly was a heavenly Father over us all, as Doralee had proclaimed until the end, then he had chosen to play the part of Father Christmas for me and had given me this gift of knowing, of being reasonably certain of who my father was.

Standing alongside Julia, hand in hand in this room of gifts, warmth, and light, it seemed almost possible to believe in God the way a child believes in Father Christmas.

Thinking of the line that Andrew delivered in the performance—"Come in, come in, and know me better, friend"—I saw myself as the trembling Scrooge, standing on the doorstep of Christmas Present. All this bounty was being opened to me, and yet I couldn't come in. Not all the way. I couldn't enter. It wasn't mine to receive.

Julia looked up at me with a different sort of "ooh!" expression. This one was along the lines of "Uh-oh, I forgot something!"

"Our stockings," she said. "I didn't look for my stocking."

My eyes went to the fireplace. No stockings hung there. They were the only key Christmas item missing from this cozy setup.

"You're right. There are no stockings hanging by the fire. Maybe Santa Claus—I mean, Father Christmas—forgot to bring them this year."

"You silly! Father Christmas doesn't hang our stockings by the fire. He hangs them on our bedposts."

"Oh. Well, then let's sneak upstairs and see if Father Christmas remembered to hang a stocking from your bedpost."

"No. I was the one who put the stocking there." Julia gave me a don't-you-know-anything look. "Father Christmas comes and puts the sweets in my stocking. I hope I get a Lion Bar this year. They're my favorite. Do you like Lion Bars?"

"I don't know. I don't think I've ever had a Lion Bar."

I could tell by her amazed expression she thought I had come from Jupiter because Jupiter had to be the only place in the universe that didn't have Lion Bars.

"If Father Christmas didn't put a Lion Bar in your stocking and if he put two in mine, I'll give you one of mine," Julia said.

Stroking her soft cheek I whispered, "Thank you."

Together we retraced our trail upstairs with more noise than we had managed on our way down. Julia raced to her room. I followed, still not sure if I was aiding and abetting a wild little tradition-breaker running free in the Whitcombe household.

When Julia pushed open her bedroom door, she gave a happy squeal, and I knew that Father Christmas had plumped up her stocking. I also heard another bedroom door open farther down the hall.

Assuming either her brother or her parents were up and about, I slipped back into my guest room and closed the door. I didn't want to be in the way.

To my surprise, Father Christmas had visited my room while I was downstairs with Julia. On one of my bedposts hung a long red sock. My name had been written with curling letters on a piece of white fabric, which was attached to the top of the stocking.

I sat on the end of the bed and examined the stocking. I had never had a Christmas stocking before. The gesture of sweet hospitality was almost too much to swallow. In the toe of the stocking was a mandarin orange that made a nice bulge and added a fresh, sweet scent to the room as I emptied all the goodies onto the top of the down comforter.

Along with the orange, my treats included a purple pen attached to a notepad, six pieces of candy (four hard pieces and two chewy), the highly praised Lion Bar (a chocolate candy bar), and a small bag of cashews.

Snuggling back under the covers, I started with the chocolate bar, remembering all the times my mother and I had dined on chocolates for our Christmas morning breakfast. The Lion Bar had a strip of caramel inside. My mother would have liked that. One bite, and I knew why it was Julia's favorite.

I moved on to the cashews and the two chewy pieces of candy. The orange I saved for last. I sucked each wedge slowly, savoring the fresh taste in my mouth. Glancing up, I caught my reflection in the large mirror above the dresser across the room. Positioning the orange slice just right, I spread my lips and flashed a wide, orange-toothed smile at my reflection.

The image made me laugh. I kept smiling and realized it had been a long, long time since I had laughed. A happy thought settled on me. Could it be that after all these years of winter in my life, it was finally, at long last, Christmas?

I dared to believe it could be so.

Chapter Fifteen

*R*emaining under the cozy down comforter, I smiled to myself, thinking of being here on Christmas morning and not alone in a London hotel room. Father Christmas had brought me something else for Christmas—being here, in this place, with these people. And I felt blissfully young.

Decisions regarding some strategic conversations would have to take place eventually. But for now I could linger, open my gifts of Christmas morning ever so slowly, and relish the lavishness of it all.

That's what I told myself as I lounged in the puffy comfort of the guest bed, gazing outside at the sunlight on the new-fallen snow.

A soft tapping came on the bedroom door. It was more like a patting than a tapping. I guessed it was Julia and called out, "Come in!"

Instead of Julia, Ellie's curious face appeared when the door opened. "So you are awake. Good morning and happy Christmas!"

"Happy Christmas to you, too."

"Julia said you showed her the snow and the presents under the tree."

"I hope that was okay." I sat up in bed.

"Yes, yes, of course it's okay. I told you to feel at home, and that's exactly what we want you to do." Ellie's hair had returned to its natural brunette shade, sans sparkles of any kind. She was wearing a plush white robe and fluffy slippers on her bare feet. The ensemble was quite a departure from the Sugarplum outfit of the evening before.

"I've come to see if you would like to join us downstairs around the tree."

I hesitated, still not sure how it could be okay for me to crash another one of their parties. "I think I'll stay here," I said. "But I would like to go to church with you later."

"Lovely!" Ellie surveyed the combat zone on my bed where all the food items had been annihilated quickly.

"Thanks for the stocking," I said, feeling shy. "I loved it, as you can see."

She smiled. "I'm sure Father Christmas would be pleased to know how much you enjoyed the gifts he left for you. Now, would you like a cup of tea, or perhaps some hot chocolate? I always make hot chocolate for the children before they open their gifts."

I smiled and nodded. "I can come down to the kitchen and get it."

"No, no, no! You stay right where you are. I'll bring it to you."

Ellie backed up and closed the door behind her before I could protest. I was still having a hard time believing her generosity. What woman with a husband and two children wouldn't consider a stray houseguest to be a burden on Christmas Day? Especially a houseguest who was a stranger?

Ellie returned with a red Christmas mug on a tray and served it to me while I was still in bed. Along with the cocoa she had brought a small croissant, a slice of well-toasted wheat bread, and a little dish of orange marmalade. I felt foolish, like a child being showered with kindness on a day she had faked an illness to play hooky from school.

"Come downstairs whenever you wish."

"Thank you."

With a flutter of her hand Ellie closed the door, but the end of her long robe got caught. Giggling, she opened the door, pulled up her robe and, with a swish, closed the door again. She may have washed away all the sparkles in her morning shower, but from where I sat, she still appeared to be a Sugarplum Fairy.

I leisurely finished my breakfast in bed and then slid back under the inviting comforter for a little doze. I was beginning to see how my mother could so easily fall into nap mode on Christmas after our breakfast of chocolates. So much chocolate at one time may release lovely endorphins, but that much sugar on an empty stomach could cause a lull, and that's exactly what it did to me.

The sleep I swam into was soothing. I dreamed of Ellie and Edward wanting me, inviting me to dine with them. The table was heavy with all sorts of wonderful things to eat. The laughter echoed off the walls, and Julia came over and climbed into my lap.

I woke and stretched. I had slept for probably only ten or fifteen minutes, but the nap had rejuvenated me. I reached into my shoulder bag beside the bed and pulled out the blue velvet pouch with the golden tassels. The photo was still there. I stared at it and knew I hadn't imagined any of this. It was the same photo as the one sitting on the mantel downstairs.

My birth certificate had been locked up long ago in a home safe in the closet of my San Francisco apartment. The folded-up playbill lay in the velvet pouch. I had a look at it and ran my eyes over words I had read many times.

"Lake Shore Community Theater Presents Shakespeare's *THE TEMPEST.*"

My mother's name was listed beside the role of Miranda. It would have been so helpful, so obvious, if the name "James Whitcombe" appeared next to one of the other characters' names. It would have all been there in black and white, and I could explain how my mother had fallen for one of the other actors, who happened to be James Whitcombe, and nine months later I had made my grand entrance onto the stage of life.

But like every other detail of my mother's life, this one wasn't that easy or that obvious.

I studied the playbill one more time. At the bottom of the paper, in small print, I read the words, "With a special thank you for the support given by the Society of Grey Hall Community Theatre."

Sitting up more fully, I read the fine print again. The Society of Grey Hall Community Theatre was the name on the plaque in front of Grey Hall where the performance had been held last night. I hadn't made the connection then.

In front of me was another small clue. Had James Whitcombe been involved in the Society of Grey Hall Community Theatre? Andrew said Sir James had contributed much to this community with his status and dedication to the theater. Had his involvement led him to the US and to this small-time community theater performance of *The Tempest?*

How was the Lake Shore Community Theater connected to the Grey Hall Community Theatre? Lake Shore group was in Michigan. I was born in Michigan and somehow ended up on the West Coast soon after. Did my mother have family in Michigan, or was she simply passing through when she joined the theater group?

It seemed that with each clue I uncovered, I picked up another string of questions. Many of those questions would never, could never, be answered. Other answers seemed to be so close, so nearly within my reach.

Tucking the photo and the playbill back into the blue velvet bag and setting it on the nightstand, I decided to venture downstairs and find a way to begin my very necessary conversation with Edward and Ellie. The evidence was mounting. I needed to say something.

I found the Whitcombe family poetically gathered around the tree. A fire blazed in the hearth. From where I stood, all the gifts appeared to have been opened. Julia was busy brushing the long hair of a new doll, and Mark, who looked tall for a twelve-year-old, stood beside his father, who was trying to fit together a control box of some sort.

"They don't exactly make this easy, do they?" Edward asked.

Ellie leaned closer. "Do you need the instructions?"

"I can get them, Father. Are they in the box?" Mark looked up and noticed my slow entrance. "Hallo. Are you Miranda?"

"Mark, mind your manners," his father said. "You should walk up to our guest, offer your hand, and introduce yourself."

Bounding past the patches of cast-aside gift wrap, Mark followed his father's instructions and came skidding up to me with a free-spirited expression that I was sure he inherited from his mother. "I am ever so pleased to make your acquaintance, madam. I am Master Mark Robert Whitcombe."

"Mark, don't be pert," Edward said.

"I'm not Pert. I'm Mark."

He received a stern look from across the room.

"Yes, Father."

"It's nice to meet you, Mark." I shook his outstretched hand. "My name is Miranda."

"My sister said you're from America, but you're not a film star."

"She's right. I am an American, but I'm not a movie star."

"Are you an actor, then?"

"No, I'm not an actor."

"Do you know any actors?"

"Yes, I have met a few."

"Really? Any ones that I would know?"

"No, none you would know."

"Mark, I have this put together now. Will you come have a look?"

Like a gazelle, the lanky twelve-year-old bounded across the room and eagerly took the controls from his father. Mark pressed a button, and out from under the camouflage of gift wrap a remote-controlled truck rumbled across the floor, heading directly for the wall. Mark used his whole body as well as his thumbs to urge the rolling vehicle to make a turn toward the center of the room.

"Well done, Mark," Ellie said.

"This is brilliant!" Mark directed the truck around a leather chair as the revved-up vehicle made a louder humming sound.

"Make it go up the wall, Markie." Julia was on her feet, watching the new toy do its stuff for the small audience.

"It doesn't go up walls. Just on floors. Don't get too close, Ju-Ju. Step back."

Ellie motioned for me to come closer to where they gathered around the tree. "If you dare," she said with a smile.

I slid onto the end of the sofa and took in the full view of the tree. Julia came over and sat beside me, showing me her new dolly and chattering about all the doll's special features, including its pony. She hopped off the couch, went for the unwrapped pony under the tree, and showed me how the doll could fit on the pony. Then Julia galloped around the room with her new toy.

Ellie shuffled the wrapping paper into a mound. Edward looked over at me and said, "Did you sleep well, Miranda?"

"Yes, very well, thank you."

"Glad to hear it. I understand you'll be joining us for church this morning."

"Yes. I hope what I'm wearing is okay for church. My luggage is still in London."

"What you're wearing will be fine," Ellie said. "You might need a warmer coat. I have several you're welcome to choose from to borrow."

"Thanks. I do need a warmer coat."

Edward seemed to be studying me. "If you don't mind, may I ask you a personal question, Miranda?"

"Certainly."

"How is it that you came to visit Carlton Heath? Our little town isn't exactly one of the usual tourist sites."

My heart beat faster. This was the opening I needed. I just hadn't prepared what to say. "I, um, I came here because—"

"Didn't Katharine say you were going to meet someone?" Ellie inserted. "Or did she say you were trying to find someone?"

"Yes," I said plainly. "I was trying to find someone."

"And how did that turn out?" Ellie asked.

This was it. This was the moment to tell Ellie and Edward who I was and why I was here. I drew in a deep breath and sat up straight.

Chapter Sixteen

*B*efore a full sentence could tumble off my lips, everyone turned to the front window, where the driveway was visible. Up to the front of the house came a large farm horse wreathed in a harness of loud jingle bells and saddled with a big red sack of wrapped gifts. Holding the reins was a merry rounded fellow with a long, flowing snowy white beard and a long robe.

"Father Christmas!" Julia shouted, leaving her doll and pony and rushing to the front window. "It's Father Christmas!"

Mark stopped pushing the buttons on the remote control and hurried to the window. Edward and Ellie exchanged surprised glances. I stood for a better view, and for the blink of a moment, I almost believed.

"Father Christmas! Father Christmas!" Julia beat her flat palm against the front window.

"Come on, Ju-Ju." Mark was already sprinting toward the door.

Ellie and Edward followed, and I was right behind. We stepped into the crisp air. Pillowed snowdrifts lined the rounded drive. As Father Christmas strode toward the children, he hitched up his robe to reveal argyle socks that I knew had to belong to Andrew.

"Happy Christmas, one and all!" Father Christmas's booming voice caused a layer of peaceful snow to quiver off a nearby tree branch and sift its way to the ground.

Bright-eyed and full of glee, Julia gave a little hop that landed her in the snow in her yellow ducky slippers. "Hallo, Father Christmas! It's me, Julia!"

Father Christmas came close and cupped her chin in his gloved hand. "And so it is!"

"We already got our presents," she proclaimed. "We've opened them. I already ate the Lion Bar. They're my favorite. Did you come back because you have more presents for us?"

"Indeed I do."

If Mark recognized Andrew, he was to be commended for keeping a straight face and playing along for the sake of his sister. However, it seemed that Mark may have been convinced that the larger-than-life man who stood before him *was* Father Christmas.

"I understand you have been a most helpful chap this year," Andrew said, doing a fair job of masking his Scottish accent.

Mark nodded.

"That's very good. Very good indeed. I happen to have a special gift here for a young man such as yourself. Young Mark, this present is for you." He reached into the red sack tied to the saddle of the old horse and handed Mark a long box that was wrapped in gold foil and tied with a big red bow.

"And for you, young Julia . . ." He hesitated, and she shivered with excitement, giving two little hops. "Ah, yes, here it is. A gift for a special young lady who has also been a good helper to her mother this year."

"Thank you, Father Christmas!" Julia took from him a box also wrapped in gold with a red ribbon.

"I have another gift here for the master of the house and his lovely wife."

"That's my mum and dad! Mummy, you get a present, too!"

The smiles on Edward and Ellie's faces as they received the gold box were more than pleasant expressions. Both of them seemed touched by what Andrew was doing for their children. The couple slipped their arms around each other, and Ellie rested her head on Edward's shoulder.

I wondered if, by this grand performance, Andrew was picking up the Father Christmas gap that had been left when Sir James passed away. Whatever the reason, Andrew's magical appearance was a gift to all of them.

"I have one more present here. Let me see. Who is this for? Oh, yes. Miranda." His rolling brogue peeked through when he said my name. I think that one slip unveiled to Mark the identity of Father Christmas, if he hadn't figured it out before. Mark was a good big brother, though, and kept the discovery to himself.

Andrew, or rather, Father Christmas, handed me a small gold box with a red ribbon. I thanked him politely and played along by adding a bit of a curtsey. Julia followed my cue and gave a curtsey as well, jiggling with joy.

"Happy Christmas to you, one and all!"

"Happy Christmas to you, Father Christmas!" Julia could barely contain herself as Andrew mounted the stout horse and urged it to trot away.

"Thank you, Father Christmas!" Mark called out as the

endearing man and his horse etched a trail in the snow down the long driveway. "Come back next year!"

"And bring me a pony!" Julia called out.

Edward and Ellie laughed.

"May I open my present now?" Julia wiggled like a jitterbug. "Please, Mummy?"

"Of course, but wouldn't you like to go inside first?"

"Yes, my feet are cold!"

We all agreed, stomped our feet, and returned to the comfy drawing room by the fire where we sat with our gifts on our laps.

Julia and Mark didn't need to be invited twice to open their gifts. Julia unwrapped a little girl's tea set and gave a squeal of delight. She immediately went to work, placing the cups and saucers on one of the end tables.

Mark pulled from his opened box a bow-and-arrow set, complete with a quiver and its long strap to position over his shoulder. His excitement was uncontainable.

Ellie and Edward exchanged glances that said, "We're going to have a talk with Andrew about this later."

"May I try it out now?" Mark asked. The strap was in place, the three arrows were in the quiver, and his feet were heading out of the room.

"Go in front of the house," Ellie said, "so we can watch you."

"And aim away from the house," Edward added.

Mark gave his parents a gleeful smirk over his shoulder, as if they should know he was mature enough to aim the arrows in the right direction without their having to tell him.

"What did Father Christmas bring you?" Julia moved toward

me, eyeing the only unopened gift left in the room. Ellie had opened the box of candy that had been given to her and Edward.

"I don't know." I shook the small box next to my ear. "I can't imagine what it could be. Can you guess?"

"I think it's a turtle," Julia said.

I smiled at her whimsical answer. "It might be. Would you help me open it?"

I handed the gift over to our expert, and she put her five-year-old fingers to fast work, peeling back the gift wrap.

"It's not a turtle." She looked up, a little disappointed. "It's only a teapot with a ribbon."

Julia dangled the dainty Christmas tree ornament in front of me.

"Lovely," Ellie said. "And fragile, isn't it, Julia? We must be careful not to drop fragile ornaments."

"I love it." I received the gift as Julia carefully placed it in my open hands. It was the first Christmas ornament I had ever been given. I found the kindness shown to me by Ellie and now by Katharine to be far beyond my ability to understand. Were all British people this trusting and generous to strangers? Or had Katharine and Ellie sensed the same inexplicable connection to me that I felt to them?

"I know where you can keep the teapot safe," Julia said.

"Where is that?"

"You could put it in your stocking. Your Christmas stocking."

"That's a good idea, Julia. I'll do that."

"If you like, I could put it in your stocking for you. That way it won't get broken, will it, Mummy?"

"That's right, darling. A stocking is a good place for a delicate ornament."

I handed over the little teapot to Julia for safekeeping. She scampered off, and Edward went over to the front window, nodding at Mark, who was ready to take aim at a tree with his bow and arrow. Ellie tidied up the room, chattering about the explosion of gift wrap being messier than in years past.

I realized this would be a good time for me to speak up. A much better time than earlier, when the children were in the room. What I had to say was for Edward and Ellie to hear.

"Keep your elbow up, Mark," Edward called out through the front window, pointing to his elbow. In a lower voice he added, "Andrew is going to have a piece of my mind before this week is out."

"He was being kind to the children. So kind. And Mark is twelve, you know."

"Of course I know he's twelve. And he's holding a better stance than I thought he would. Has he done archery before?"

"Last summer. At the Culliford's lawn party. Do you remember how young Anna challenged Mark and the other boys to an archery contest and then bested them all?"

"Oh, yes, that's right. I had forgotten about that." Edward waved and nodded at his son, as Mark made an improved shot that glanced off the side of the tree trunk. "It might be all right after all. He does have the posture, doesn't he?"

"He's your son." Ellie sent a soft smile across the room to her husband's back.

A brief pause hovered over us, and I opened my lips to speak. Nothing came out. I began to tremble. Swallowing and stepping over to the fireplace, I reached up for the framed picture. Gathering all my courage, I tried to speak again, this time with a visual aid.

"Edward, Ellie, I wanted to say something to you both, and now seems like a good time."

They turned to face me.

I smiled.

Go ahead. Tell them.

As my lips parted, Julia skipped into the room. "Miranda, is this yours? This little blue pillow?"

Chapter Seventeen

*J*ulia, no!" I nearly dropped the framed photograph in my hand as I rushed to snatch the blue velvet purse away from startled Julia. Her lower lip quivered.

"It's all right," I said quickly. It didn't appear that she had opened the purse. "I was surprised to see you with this, that's all. I didn't mean to frighten you."

"Julia, it's not polite to touch other people's belongings," Edward said with a fatherly firmness.

Realizing I was still holding the frame, I took the admonition along with Julia and returned the photo to its rightful place on the mantel.

"Sorry, Miranda," Julia said in a small voice.

"It's okay, sweetie." My voice came out light and softer. I smiled in her direction, and she seemed to perk up. "Really, honey, don't feel bad."

"Julia loves to help out, don't you, darling?" Ellie went to her daughter and gave her some reassuring pats. Looking at me Ellie added, "She's forever fetching items for me. Coats and purses. Is everything all right, then?"

"Yes, fine. Sorry I jumped the way I did."

"Don't worry. It's all right. Julia, why don't you set up a tea party for us? Would you like that?"

Julia gave a timid nod and went to the end table where her tiny tea set was waiting.

"Shall I pour, or will you?" Ellie asked.

"I'll pour, silly Mummy. It's my party." Julia cast a shy glance at me.

I smiled, hoping my outburst hadn't ruined the closeness I had felt with Julia earlier.

She looked at her tea set and then back at me. "Would you like to come to my tea party, too?"

"Yes, I would like to come very much."

"Then you can sit right there." She went to work pouring invisible tea into one of the four cups.

The three of us "ladies," as Julia now called us, sipped our invisible tea while Edward remained at the window, watching his pajama-wearing son shoot another arrow into the air.

"It's a wonder he isn't frozen solid yet." Ellie glanced over her shoulder at Mark. "We should call him inside, though. We do need to get ready for the Christmas service."

Edward left the room, and Ellie excused herself from the tea party, thanking her hostess before turning back into the mother and sending Julia upstairs to dress for church. I offered to help in any way I could. Ellie assured me there was nothing more to do.

"The turkey is already in the oven," she said. "I've managed to organize everything this year, so I think there's only one thing for you to do, and this is only if you would like, because I can certainly do it later. But the cutlery needs to be laid out on the dining table."

I assumed she meant I could set the table with the silver-ware, but I didn't see a dining-room table in the drawing room.

"It's all on the sideboard in the dining room, which is the room directly across from the study. I can show you now, if you'd like."

Clutching the blue purse, I followed Ellie into the dining room where she showed me how she wanted the table to be set. The china plates were a cheerful seasonal pattern with sprigs of holly and bright red berries circling the edges. Each of the twelve places had a dinner plate and a bread plate. Silverware of all shapes and sizes accompanied the various plates and needed to be positioned on the table just so.

Down the center of the ivory tablecloth ran a winding swath of fresh evergreen boughs. The fragrance enlivened the rather small formal dining room. Tea candles were tucked here and there, ready to give a soft glow when the time came for the Christmas feast. Over the table hung a simple chandelier with red and green ribbons entwined around the dangling crystals.

Edward appeared in the doorway. "Ellie, did you have a chance to give one last look to the papers on the desk?"

"No, I didn't. Do you need to make the decision today, or can you wait?"

"I can wait, of course, but I will be seeing Robert at the service this morning. He is eager for an answer, you know. After the party last night, he and I put our best efforts into the discussion, but I'm afraid we have failed to come to an agreement."

"Right." Ellie handed me the forks. "The papers are still on the desk?"

"Yes."

"I'll come have a look. Then we really must dress for church."

Ellie and her husband stepped into the study across the hall.

I could hear their voices but didn't think they realized how clearly their words carried from room to room.

"It does seem, Edward, that finding this paper in your father's wallet should be reason enough to include it in the collection."

"Robert would agree with you, of course. I was only hoping for some possible clarification."

"What we really need is a fresh pair of eyes on this," Ellie said.

I heard Edward's brisk footsteps returning to the dining room. He stuck out his jaw and looked at me through the lower portion of his glasses. His stance reminded me of a scientist examining a rare bug. "Are you by any chance good at word games, Miranda?"

"Not especially."

"Pity." He sighed. "Would you mind coming and having a look anyway? We have a small problem with a short poem."

Mystified, I followed him across the hall into the study. In front of us was the fabulous, wide desk. The top of the desk was covered with papers that seemed to have been placed in a specific order. The handwriting on all the pages matched. Some of the pages were filled with words and spaced like a handwritten letter. Other pages had only a few words. Even though the pages were upside down from where I stood, I could see the consistent slant of the author's penmanship.

"It's this one." Ellie pointed to a piece of paper in the far corner. The page at one time had been folded into a small rectangle and was now yellowed along the many creases.

"We're trying to make a final decision on several pieces of my father's works, which are under consideration by the British Theatrical Preservation League for a historical collection. We're certain the piece in question is in his handwriting. It matches all the other pieces. However, this poem simply doesn't follow the pattern or logic of his other works."

"In other words, none of us understands what the poem means," Ellie said.

"We believe it was an original piece and not copied from a quote. The challenge is that we're being asked to provide some reference data and, quite frankly, we're puzzled. If there is a meaning to the piece, it certainly has escaped us."

By that point in the conversation, my heart was pounding. These were my father's papers. I was looking at his letters, in his handwriting.

Stepping to the other side of the desk, I held my racing pulse in check as I read the five lines that solidified my birthright.

by lake shore in moon glow
first time only time
as it was at the beginning of time
beguiling eve once
now ever in this failed heart

I knew what the poem meant.

I knew all about the moonlit night beside a lake on a feathery bed of moss. James Whitcombe slept there with beguiling Eve Carson, the actress, and the memory of her had never left him. It was the first time, the only time, he was unfaithful to his wife. My mother had taken the photo from his wallet, and in its place he had inserted this small clue. A poem. An ode to beguiling Eve, and perhaps a temperate reminder to his failed vow of faithfulness.

"It's a mystery." Ellie shook her head. "I'm not sure anyone can explain the meaning. Apparently, it was special to him. That is the part we can choose to honor."

I clenched my jaw, hoping my expression wouldn't give away any of the emotions that came rushing forth. Long ago I had chosen to believe in my father. After seeing the photo, seeing the name of his community theater on the playbill, and hearing this poem, I knew my father was real. His name was Sir James Whitcombe. The sweetest part about these words, written in my father's hand, was that my mother had meant something to him. He had carried a memory of her in his wallet.

"Any thoughts, Miranda?" Edward turned to me with his bug-examining expression.

I hesitated far too long. Edward and Ellie stared at me until I finally spoke, my voice cracking as I said, "I think the poet was writing about a woman. The woman was named Eve. He wanted to remember her."

By the stunned expressions on their faces, I knew they never had considered the possibility that the "eve" in the poem might be a person and not a reference to the time of day.

Ellie read the words again and shook her head. "That couldn't be right. If it's a love poem, the name would be Margaret. Not Eve. He and Margaret were married for fifty-eight years. He wrote a number of poems to her."

Obviously, James had experienced a season, or perhaps only a moment, with Eve. I was the living proof of that.

"Maybe," I said gingerly, "your father had a moment, so to speak, with another woman, and—"

Before I could finish, Edward brusquely squared his shoulders. "That's not possible."

"It's certainly not probable." Ellie gave me a sympathetic expression the way one would look at an outsider who didn't know anything. "We do appreciate your willingness to offer an opinion. That is why we asked you. But, you see, that possibility is not probable."

"Not at all probable," Edward stated firmly. "Not probable and certainly not possible."

"But she wouldn't know that, Edward, because, after all . . ." Turning to me, Ellie said kindly, "You didn't know Edward's father."

Clenching my jaw and looking away I said, "You're right. I didn't know him."

"We'd best be getting ready for church, Edward."

The two of them turned to leave the study, but I longed to stay where I was, right there, in the midst of my father's letters.

Edward stopped at the doorway and cleared his throat.

I looked up and with my bravest smile said, "Would it be all right if I stayed in here?"

"Certainly," Ellie answered. "It's a wonderful room, isn't it?"

"Would it also be all right if I had a look at the rest of these papers?" I knew my request was bold, but I longed to touch something my father had touched. I knew these papers might be the only chance I would have to glimpse his heart.

Ellie looked to Edward for his answer to my strange question.

"You're not a reporter or anything, are you?"

"No, I'm not a reporter."

I'm not a lot of things. But I am the daughter of Sir James Whitcombe, whether you think such a thing is possible or probable or not.

I waited a moment. Did I only think that, or did I say it aloud? Edward and Ellie didn't look shocked. I must have only thought it. How disastrous if that declaration had slipped out.

Edward looked at Ellie's kind eyes and then back at me. "I don't mind your having a look as long as everything remains as it is." As an afterthought he added, "We've nothing to hide."

Chapter Eighteen

e left in a flurry for the Christmas morning service. Julia sat beside me in the car's backseat. Holding my hand, she chattered like a little bird. I was glad for her prattle because it meant Edward and Ellie weren't compelled to converse with me about what else I might have seen in the letters in the study.

Most of the papers were cordial correspondence, thanking a colleague for a dinner invitation or a theater critic for a good review. One of the letters was a note to his brother Robert, expressing appreciation for a pocketknife Robert had bought James on a trip to Switzerland in 1975.

One other poem in the collection, the one that referred to "Margaret of the Midnight Sun," preoccupied my thoughts as we drove to church.

> *you touch*
> *with light*
> *the arctic hollow of my*
> *pilgrim soul*
> *margaret of the midnight sun*
> *with you*

i journey through always summer
and never night

The poem opened my mind to the depth of Sir James's love
for his wife Margaret. It made me dwell on the thought that he
had no business sleeping with my mother.

He had a wife. He loved her. What was he doing allowing himself to be
"beguiled" by Eve?

I was aware of a sense of guilt simply for being born. I felt
bad about being the result of my mother's "moment" with a married man. I never had felt remorse because I hadn't known any
details surrounding my existence. My mother's choice not to tell
me about my father had kept me from lingering over such possible
revelations. Her silence had kept me buoyant on a sea of secrecy.

I looked down at Julia's little hand in mine and knew that no
child should ever be handed the self-destructive seed of feeling
guilty for being born. None of us gets to select our parents.
How can any of us feel responsible for coming into this world?
It wasn't my idea to be born.

I remembered a conversation I'd had with Doralee when she
was trying to find my father the second time. I told her my life
must have been an accident. My guess, I said, was that my mom
must have done something that "put her on God's bad side," and
that's why she didn't want me or anyone to know who my father
was. We were cursed.

Doralee got pretty revved up and said my life was *not* an
accident. She said all of us start life "on God's bad side," under a
curse. She said we all need someone who will make things right
for us with God.

That's how she explained Jesus to me. He was the only one since Adam and Eve who wasn't locked into the curse when he was born.

"God is supreme," she told me. "Your life was no mistake, Miranda. God can do whatever he wants. Isn't it obvious he wants you?"

At the time I said I much preferred the premise that I was an accident of nature and in control of my own destiny. At least my destiny in this life. After that, I wasn't sure what happened.

Julia gave my hand a gentle squeeze, checking to make sure I was still listening to her chatter. I gave her little hand a squeeze back and decided that going to church on Christmas morning felt right, as if a part of me was saying to God, "All right, I'm here. Go ahead. Show me what you've got. This is your chance. Prove to me that I'm not a fluke of evolution."

I didn't mean those words in a disrespectful way. I was looking for affirmation. Much like Julia squeezing my hand, I wanted to know if God was paying attention and if he would squeeze back.

As I became more curious about what awaited me at the church service, we arrived at the same charming village chapel I had walked past the night before. Sunlight spilled over the top of the spire and warmed the quilted earth that trailed from the rose bed and covered the quarried gravestones. The image was glorious. If ever I felt in the mood to set foot inside a church, this was the morning.

We arrived early because Mark and Julia had parts in the Christmas service. Julia was jumping up and down on one foot by the time we filed through the arched entrance. The inside of the stone church felt as chilly as the outside. Small electrical heaters were plugged into a long orange extension cord. The metal grates were glowing red, huffing and puffing out their heat in an effort to warm the cavernous space.

Ellie took the children to where they were to report for their part in the service. Edward and I filed into a wooden pew four rows from the church's front. I kept my coat on after I sat down. Actually, the coat was Ellie's and much warmer than mine. It came past my knees, and the collar was made from white rabbit fur, warming my neck and shoulders luxuriously. I was grateful that none of the well-dressed worshippers could see my casual apparel under the coat. On the outside, thanks to Ellie, I fit in.

As others from the village entered the church and took their seats, I looked around the sanctuary. The church was designed with the same feel of ornate Victorian splendor as the theater the night before. A variety of textures dominated the floor, ceiling, and walls. The stained-glass windows along the sides of the chapel seemed to come alive in the morning light, showing off the tranquil expressions of the subjects.

I gazed at all four of the tall windows that balanced each other on the sides of the chapel. I didn't know who any of the people were supposed to be. Doralee would have known. Aside from Mary and Joseph, the only biblical character I was familiar with was Christ.

His image was the central figure in a stained-glass window at the front of the chapel, behind the altar. The representation was Anglo-Saxon looking, which I found amusing. The artist who designed the stained-glass window had given the Christ figure long, flowing blond hair. That seemed odd to me since I

Robin Jones Gunn

knew Jesus lived in the Middle East and therefore would have
had dark features.

I liked everything else about the window. Christ was portrayed as a ruling king seated on a throne. Instead of appearing
aloof in his majesty, this Jesus had a compelling expression. His
arms were extended out in a gesture of invitation. Clearly visible were red pieces of stained glass strategically placed where
the nails had been driven through his wrists.

With the sunshine so perfectly centered behind the front
of the church, the emblazoned image of Christ shone with a
golden intensity. I didn't have the impression that he might
lunge across the open expanse and devour me, like a one-eyed
dragon might. Instead, his open arms reminded me of how wel-
coming Andrew was when he greeted me at the Tea Cosy with,
"Come in, come in, and know me better, friend."

Ellie slid into the pew next to me and gave my arm a pat. I
smiled at her, but all I wanted to do was shrink down into the
warm coat. I felt the fur come up to my ears. As warm as the
coat made me feel, I couldn't suppress a rising sense of discomfort that started in my stomach and worked its way to the top
of my head. I knew this discomfort. I had felt it the day I had
decided to believe in my father. That day all the old myths
were abolished. The new belief took over. And that belief in my
father had been true.

Adjusting my posture, I reminded myself that if—and only
if—I was going to believe in God, I would have to let go of some
strongly held presuppositions to make way for the supernatural.
Then I remembered all the coincidences since I had arrived in
England and how they begged for an explanation. Along with

these coincidences was all the kindness I was being shown for no earthly reason. Could any of this have to do with God?

An even more unsettling thought came over me, intensifying my discomfort. Could it be that God was the one who had offered the first squeeze of my hand, so to speak, and now it was my turn to squeeze back?

A woman wearing a red floral shawl over a simple black dress stepped up to the front of the church with a violin and bow in her hand. The congregation hushed as she tucked the polished instrument under her chin and played. Her passion for her music was evident. This was not a production. She felt what she was playing, and it flowed from her fingertips. The beauty of her expression was something I hadn't expected to see or experience in a church.

At the end of her piece, a man who had been standing to the side took the last note she played and began to sing a capella. The words that rolled from his deep chest were of the omnipotent God and included the words, "Wonderful," "Counselor," "Everlasting Father," and "Prince of Peace."

He concluded with a long note that resonated with such depth that it seemed to warm the pews. Stepping to the side, he made way for four children, including Mark and Julia, to tromp down the center aisle. The children took their places. Julia looked adorable in her red and white Christmas dress and red rubber rain boots. She held her hands behind her back and grinned widely at her mom. Mark stood tall and unsmiling, looking straight ahead. He was wearing a robe over his clothes and a fancy silk turban on his head.

The first boy in the lineup was dressed as a beggar with

appropriate soot smudges on his face. He took a step forward and in a blaring voice shouted, "'My Gift' by Christina Rossetti. 'What can I give Him, poor as I am?'" He stepped back in place.

The next boy stepped forward holding a shepherd's staff. He also was wearing a robe. "'If I were a shepherd I would bring a lamb.'" He held up a stuffed lamb the size of a football.

Mark stepped forward with all the dash and drama that must run in his veins and said with perfect inflection, "'If I were a wise man I would do my part.'"

He stepped back.

Julia was still looking around, hands behind her back, grinning at every parishioner she recognized.

Whispering from the side of his mouth, Mark urged his sister forward.

She took a big step in her oversized boots. Swallowing and extending her round little chin, she said her line with sweetness. "'Yet, what can I give Him? Give my heart.'" From behind her back, she pulled out a big red Valentine-shaped heart and held it for all to see.

The congregation's approval was instant, though formal. If it's possible to "feel" a room of people smiling, that's what I felt.

Mark and Julia wedged into the pew with us. Mark sat next to his father, and Julia squeezed in between Ellie and me. She held the red heart in her lap with great care and swung her crossed ankles demurely. It was evident that the little star was quite pleased.

A minister took his position behind the carved wooden pulpit and read from an enormous book. I soon guessed it to be the

Bible because the passage was about shepherds abiding in the fields at night to keep watch over the sheep. I recognized the story from watching a rerun of the old *A Charlie Brown Christmas* a few years ago on TV. One of the cartoon characters, I think it was Linus, recited the same lines about how an angel appeared and told the shepherds not to be afraid. Unto them was born that day a child. The angels sang. The shepherds hurried to Bethlehem where they found Mary and Joseph and the baby, who was lying in a manger.

My gaze rose to the stained-glass image of Christ, who was seated as a ruler. The Prince of Peace, with his arms extended in an invitation. Accessible. Willing to make things right with me before omnipotent God.

Access to a father. My father. That was all I ever longed for.

My eyes teared up.

The minister concluded the reading, and the congregation stood. I stood with them. The minister recited a prayer. "Our Father, who art in heaven, hallowed be thy name."

Everyone around me joined in and recited the lyrical prayer, but I didn't. I didn't know the words. That's because he was their Father, not mine. They could climb up on his strong shoulders and make daring leaps into the mysterious depths without fear. They had the relationship. I did not. And yet, I was invited to come.

Blinking away my tears, I stared across the watery distance. There, at the deep end of the church, the golden Savior seemed to be staring back at me.

I didn't move. Neither did he.

Chapter Nineteen

On the drive back to the house after the Christmas service, I kept blinking. I'd gone too deep at church. Too deep into the mystery of all that couldn't be explained. It felt as if we were driving away from a singular presence and I was dripping with whatever the spiritual equivalent might be of pool chlorine. It would be too easy for him to follow my trail. I wanted Edward to drive faster before the golden-eyed Savior came after me.

Closing and bolting the door of my heart, I didn't peek out to see if he was still there. Instead, I pressed all my thoughts to picturing how I would finish this day. A sketchy plan formulated. First, I would draw Edward aside before Christmas dinner was served. I would lay out the facts for him, even though he wouldn't want to hear what I had to say. I would show him the poem, the photo, and the playbill and tell him the name that appeared on my birth certificate. I would put the information out there. That was fair.

Then I would leave. I would return to the London hotel. If Edward wanted to tell his wife or anyone else, it would be his choice. If he wanted to contact me before I left London, I would leave the name of the hotel with him.

That way I wouldn't intrude any longer on this family. If Edward chose not to believe me or take into account the evidence, it didn't matter. I knew. I had received what I came all this way to find.

We arrived back at the house, and the children moaned that the snow was melting. Edward said he would take them into the back garden to build a snowman and sent them upstairs to change into what he called their "woolies."

I knew that would give me the ten minutes I needed alone with Edward before slipping out of the house and returning to London. Ellie would understand. I knew she would.

In an effort to put all the mannerly pieces in their proper places, as we climbed out of the car, I said to Ellie, "Thank you so much for your hospitality. I especially appreciate the handkerchief you gave me. Are you sure it's okay if I keep it?"

She waved her hand. "Oh yes. Definitely. I have quite a few. My mother-in-law has been embroidering them for years."

"Margaret?" I asked. "Your mother-in-law, Margaret, embroidered the handkerchief?"

"Yes. It's a bit of a hobby for her, really. She paints as well. You'll meet her this afternoon when she arrives. You'll love her. She's a beautiful person."

I stopped in my slushy tracks. "Margaret is coming here? This afternoon?"

"Yes, of course. She lives here with us, you know. She went to Bedford for a few days to be with Edward's sister, Marion, for Christmas Eve. They usually come here, Marion and Gordon and their brood, but this year they decided to huddle close to the home fires. Margaret is an absolute sweetheart. You'll see."

"I didn't know she was still alive."

"Oh yes, very much alive."

My plan to disclose my secret and then flee now seemed like a bad idea. It was one thing to tell a grown man his father had been unfaithful. That was stunning enough. To reveal to an elderly widow that I was the result of her husband's indiscretion thirty years earlier . . . it felt cruel.

Ellie stepped into the house and looked at me over her shoulder. "Are you coming in? I'm going to get straight to work in the kitchen, and I will tell you now, I absolutely don't allow anyone in there when I'm creating. I'm rather selfish that way. I hope you understand. I will accept assistance on the cleanup, though."

She grinned and set off for the kitchen.

I stepped in under the "Grace and Peace Reside Here" motto and closed the front door. Alone in the entryway, I thought that leaving right then sounded like a good choice. The best choice. No one in Carlton Heath needed to know. Ever.

However, Katharine knew. I knew she knew. If Edward, Ellie, or Margaret ever heard of this missing piece of Sir James's life, it shouldn't come to them because Katharine felt compelled to speak up after I had gone. That wouldn't be fair to the Whitcombes or Katharine, either.

I also knew that Katharine and Andrew were still planning to come to Christmas dinner because they had discussed what they were bringing when we chatted in the church after the service. I was feeling hemmed in.

Climbing the stairs to the privacy of the guestroom, I entered and closed the door. My exhaustion was real as I stretched out on the bed. I had been in England for only twenty-four hours, yet everything in my heart and life had spun off into another galaxy.

"What should I do?" I whispered. "What should I do?"

I rolled over on the bed, and a beam of winter sunlight slipped through the thickpaned window and touched the side of my face.

I bolted upright and looked around.

He was here. He had followed me into this room, through the closed door. Not literally followed me, of course, but I knew he was there all the same. He hadn't stayed on his stained-glass throne. He had come to me and was with me now. I couldn't shake him.

"What do you want?" I whispered in a trembling voice.

All was silent. Peacefully silent except for the pounding of my heart. And in my heart I knew why he was there. I knew what he wanted. Wasn't it obvious, as Doralee had said? He wanted me.

Inside the silence, surrounded by the mystery, I spoke the single word that had been lying in wait all these years. "Father."

His name tasted like golden syrup on the tip of my tongue.

I remained still. Very still.

The only sound I heard was Mark and Julia shouting and squealing as they played in the snow in the back garden. A moment later I heard another sound. Loud, cheerful voices echoed in the entryway. Doors opened and closed. I heard Ellie's laughter. Margaret had arrived.

I didn't want to go downstairs. I didn't want to meet Margaret. I didn't want the woman who had shared her life with

Sir James Whitcombe for fifty-eight years to look into my eyes and note that they were clear and blue like her husband's.

I wanted to evaporate. To turn into a snowflake, fly out the bedroom window, and melt in the arms of some inconspicuous shrub.

But an unfamiliar sense of hope covered me and coaxed me out of my fear. He was still here. He hadn't left me alone. Even though I had spoken no specific words nor understood entirely what had transpired, relinquishing my heart to him had been distinct and fixed forever. He had come to me, and I had folded myself into his greatness. I believed.

A light tapping on the guest-room door kicked my heartbeat up a notch or two. I didn't respond. The knock repeated.

"Miranda?" It was Andrew's voice, his Scottish brogue rolling the "r."

"Yes?"

"Ah! Miranda, I've been sent to invite you to come downstairs and join the festivities."

Without moving from the bed, I timidly called out, "Andrew?"

"Still here," he replied from behind the closed door.

"Who else is here?"

"Katharine is downstairs, if that's what you're asking."

"Anyone else?"

"Ah! You're wondering if my son has arrived yet. You can put yourself at ease. For the time being, the only MacGregors downstairs would be Katharine and myself. Now, shall I tell Ellie you'll be joining us, or are you looking for a little peace and quiet?"

"I'll . . . I'll be down in a few minutes."

I looked up just in time to see an arrow hit the window and drop to the ground. Sliding off the bed I hurried across the room, expecting to see Mark with a grimace on his face.

Instead, I looked down on Edward, who stood with the bow still in his hand. His surprise was evident. Mark appeared equally stunned. By the way the two of them were positioned, they seemed to have aimed for the apple tree in the opposite direction of the house. How did the arrow manage to flip back and hit the window?

I waved and offered a smile, trying to let them know that all was well. Except for a tiny crack that appeared in the beveled glass, the window was still intact.

Julia, who had been standing to the side with her mittened hands over her mouth, waved at me, calling out something I couldn't hear.

Edward put down the bow and offered a sheepish shrug. The children then laughed along with their father, and I felt overcome with a bittersweetness. This family was a cohesive unit. Each had his or her place. My intrusion worked as long as I was the foreign stranger whom they had taken pity on and invited in for the holidays.

That's what I wanted to remain to them. A stranger. Not the illegitimate daughter of Sir James, their beloved patriarch.

Slipping the teapot ornament out of the Christmas stocking, I tucked it into my shoulder bag and prepared to make a beeline for the front door. Grace and peace did reside here. I refused to be the one to disrupt that blessing.

Chapter Twenty

*J*made it as far as the bottom of the stairs. Katharine met me there, saw my shoulder bag, and quietly began her "che-che-che" sounds, as if I were a frightened bird and she could calm me.

"I need to go," I told her in a low voice, trying to sound as firm as I could.

She didn't move.

"It's not fair to them, Katharine. I found what I came for, and that's enough. They don't need to know."

Her expression was compassionate yet reluctant to agree with me.

"Katharine, I know that you know. I saw it in your eyes last night. I'm begging you, please, please, don't say anything to anyone, ever. I want to leave this place and this family just as they are. Will you promise me, Katharine? Promise me you will never say anything?"

"I cannot promise you that, Miranda. I'm sorry."

"Why?" I felt panic rising in me. Katharine was the only obstacle in my path. Why couldn't she see the urgency of and the clear reasoning for keeping my secret? "Have you already told someone? Did you tell Andrew?"

"No, I haven't said anything. I believe it's your place to open this gift."

"But it's not a gift, Katharine. It's a bomb. It's a tangled mess. It's—"

"It's the truth, Miranda. That's all it is. The truth."

"Okay, it's the truth. Don't we all know that the truth can hurt others too much sometimes?"

She dipped her chin in acknowledgement of my statement, but she wouldn't leave it there. "And sometimes after the hurt, the truth heals."

I knew the longer I stood there, the less likely I could slip out of the house unnoticed. Pressing in closer to Katharine I begged her, "Do not tell. Please. This isn't your secret to share with anyone. This is my life. Please. Keep this secret for me. They don't need to know, Katharine."

Her lips remained pursed, but her eyes welled with tears. "I can't promise you that."

Anger flamed up inside me, turning my face red as I pushed past her and strode toward the front door. Her unreasonableness was forcing my hand. Fine. I would tell Edward. But not face to face. He would have the truth in writing. The letter would arrive after Christmas. After I had flown back to San Francisco. That would only be fair to him.

Too flustered to even say good-bye to Katharine, I reached for the handle and flung open the door. Then I realized I wasn't sure how to get to the train station. If I could reach the church we went to this morning, I could probably get there. But even if I remembered the way to the church, I couldn't walk that far in the slushy snow.

To add to my humiliation, I wasn't sure how to place a call on a British phone to arrange cab service. Did "411" work on the other side of the pond?

I needed help.

Closing the heavy front door with a thud, I slowly turned around, knowing that Katharine would still be there.

I spoke firmly without looking at her. "Would you please tell me how to call for a taxi?"

Ellie popped into the entry hall, wiping her hands on an apron that covered the front of her outfit. "I thought I heard the door. Has someone else arrived?"

"No," Katharine said.

"If the children come in through the front, would you two make sure they leave their wet things by the radiator?"

Before bopping back into the kitchen, Ellie looked at the two of us standing in our tense positions and cautiously asked, "Is everything all right?"

"I need to use your phone, if you don't mind."

"Not at all. Would you like to use the one in the study?"

"Yes, thank you."

I was about to slide past Katharine when she said, "It would be better if you stayed, Miranda. It really would."

Before I could respond, the latch jiggled on the front door. Two people entered. First came a round, rosy woman with fair skin, white hair, and wire-rimmed glasses. She was dressed in a long coat with a matching fur-lined hat, and she carried a Harrods shopping bag in her leather-gloved hand.

The other person was a uniformed chauffeur who was carrying two small pieces of luggage.

"Hello, hello!" the cheery woman greeted us. She motioned for the driver to put the luggage in the corner and then pulled her gloves off finger by finger.

Katharine and Ellie went to the woman and greeted her warmly. I hung back, stunned.

Could this be Margaret?

I had expected the wife of Sir James to be tall and elegant and to fill the room with the fragrance of Chanel perfume upon her entrance. This woman who chuckled merrily and exuded the essence of cinnamon rolls didn't seem like the wife of a famous actor. If this was Margaret, then she had turned out to be everything my mother was not.

"You must meet Miranda." Ellie stepped back so the woman could have a look at me. "She's our special guest all the way from America. Miranda, this is Margaret, my mother-in-law. Margaret Whitcombe."

Propelled by the few manners I had left in me, I stepped toward her, keeping my gaze diverted. I didn't want Margaret to look into my eyes.

"Lovely to meet you," she said. "Welcome and happy Christmas."

"Thank you. Merry Christmas to you, too. You have a beautiful home."

"That's kind of you to say."

I could feel Katharine's gaze on me, but I couldn't say anything else. I didn't know what to say. I was thinking about the driver, who was standing only a few feet away. He had a car waiting out front. More than likely he would be willing to drive me wherever I wanted to go for the right price. All I had to do was open my mouth and say something.

Yet I remained silent, caught off guard in the unexpectedness of the moment.

As soon as Margaret had removed her coat and hat, she settled her account with the driver. I knew this was my chance to arrange a ride, but as I looked at him, nothing came out of my mouth. The driver left, and I stood there as a victim of my own sabotage. Either that or I was being compelled by something larger than myself.

I somehow found it easy to believe it was the latter.

"Your timing is perfect," Ellie said to her mother-in-law, taking her coat from her. "We're just about ready to eat. The children are in the back with Edward and Andrew. You won't believe this, but Andrew arrived at the house this morning dressed as Father Christmas. He had the Bromleys' old horse decked out in bells. The children were enchanted."

"It must have been lovely," Margaret said. "Did the children recognize Andrew?"

"Julia believed Andrew was the real Father Christmas. I'm not sure about Mark. The whole thing was quite touching for Edward. He told me he remembered all the years his father had played that role and how grand it was of Andrew to pick up the tradition now with our children. Really, Katharine, it was exceptionally good of Andrew to surprise us all that way."

"You must know," Katharine added, "that Andrew was much more excited about it than the children or even Edward could have been."

"I'm sorry now that I missed all the happenings around here," Margaret said. "It sounds as if you had a lovely Christmas morning."

"The best," Ellie said. "And what about you? How is everything with Marion and Gordon and the rest of them? Are you tired from the drive?"

"I'm not at all weary, thank you. Is there anything I can do to help with the dinner?"

"No, not a thing for you to do. The turkey is nearly ready, but you know how particular I am about presentation. We should be able to sit down in about twenty minutes. Will that work for you?"

"Yes, of course. Do keep in mind that I am available for assistance if you need me. I'll take my luggage to my room. Marion and the others all send their love, by the way."

"Oh Miranda, would you mind helping her lift those?" Ellie asked.

"They aren't heavy," Margaret protested.

"Nevertheless, you shouldn't be lifting them," Ellie said. "And Katharine, I wonder if you might be willing to go to the dining room for me, light all the candles, and then help arrange the nibbles before the children come dashing inside."

Katharine sent a final comforting glance my direction before going to fulfill her duty in the dining room. I returned an appreciative expression. *Grace and peace,* I kept saying to myself. *Grace and peace.*

My shoulder bag was still over my arm, positioned and ready for my exit. Instead of heading for the door, I reached for Margaret's small suitcases and found them light and easy to carry.

"How awfully kind of you." Margaret headed to the left, toward the study. "My room is just this way. It's not far."

I followed close behind, knowing only one thing for certain. Ever since I had arrived in Carlton Heath, nothing had gone the way I had expected—not that I had any ideas about what should happen. But it seemed that every time I made a small effort to move forward, the next step would come rushing to meet me. So at this point, I figured I should keep making my small efforts and see what happened next.

A distinct impression continued to rest on me: I was not alone.

Chapter Twenty-One

Margaret led me down the hall past the study on the left and the dining room on the right. We walked by what appeared to be another bedroom on the left. To the right was a series of small rectangular windows positioned at eye level. A small pink rosebud was painted in the center of each window. I could guess who the artist was.

Pausing, Margaret looked out one of the windows. The view opened to the garden where the children were throwing snowballs at each other with the remnants of the quickly melting snow. I noticed that Andrew was now the one with the bow and arrow. He was wearing slacks and a thick sweater instead of his kilt. Edward stood close, appearing to be intently giving instructions to Andrew, who looked quite confident without Edward's assistance.

"Someone received a new toy," Margaret said with a grin.

"The bow and arrow were Mark's gift from Father Christmas," I said.

"Oh, I'm sure they were." I noted a twinkle in Margaret's eye. She caught my eye for a moment. I looked away.

We continued down the long hall, heading for the room at the far end. Next to the room was a door that opened to the back garden. As we passed that door, it swung open and in came Julia, squealing.

A poorly aimed snowball followed Julia through the door and hit the wrong target.

"Grandmother!" Julia cried. "Mark, you hit Grandmother!"

I dropped the suitcases and rushed to Margaret's side. The airy snowball already had begun to melt off her surprised face. She straightened her glasses and brushed off her cheek.

Julia stood in front of her grandmother, both hands over her mouth, her eyes wide. "Sorry, Grandmother! Sorry!"

"It's all right, Julia dear. Quite all right. Nothing broken. That in itself is a small accomplishment at my age."

I noticed then that Margaret was bleeding from the side of her mouth. Julia noticed as well.

"Blood! Markie, you made Grandmother bleed!"

"You must have bitten your lip." I reached into my shoulder bag and found the travel packet of tissues I had fumbled around for last night at the theater. Pulling out a tissue, I handed it to Margaret.

She looked at me as she dabbed the corner of her mouth. I should have looked away. I planned all along to look away, as I had done earlier with her. But when Margaret's eyes met mine, I returned the gaze.

"Mark, come here and apologize to your grandmother at once," Edward's stern voice called as he joined us by the open door. A chilly December breeze raced past us and went frolicking down the hallway.

Mark came forward and politely said, "I'm awfully sorry, Grandmother."

"Nothing to worry about. It was an accident, Mark. Now, do take off your boots before coming inside."

Mark did as she asked and padded down the hallway in his wet wool socks, leaving footprints as he went.

"Welcome home, Mother." Edward stepped up and gave her a kiss on the cheek. "Nothing like making an event of your homecoming, wouldn't you say?"

"Yes indeed."

"I can take it from here," Edward said to me as he picked up his mother's suitcases and escorted the luggage and Margaret to the room at the end of the hall.

Julia slipped her cold, mittened hand in mine. "Do you want to come outside and help me make a snowman?"

"I can help you for a few minutes, but your mother said it's almost time to eat."

"Are the nibbles ready?"

"I think so."

"Then I'm coming in now!" She kicked off her boots, pulled off her mittens, and wiggle-walked out of her coat.

I closed the side door to the garden, hung up Julia's coat on the hallway peg, and followed her to the dining room. Everything was ready for a grand celebration in the candlelit room. Anticipation glowed in the candles' reflection on the stemware and the shiny china plates.

"Mummy said I could sit by you so I can help you with your cracker."

I smiled my appreciation at Julia even though I wasn't sure why I would need help to eat a cracker. Sliding my shoulder bag inconspicuously under the chair she assigned to me, I drew in the scent of the bayberry candles and thought about what might happen next. I wasn't sure what I was going to do, but I knew I couldn't bolt just yet.

The rest of the clan found its way into the dining room, and everyone stood around sampling the appetizers and making small talk. I stood to the side and listened. The mix of all the voices with their British accents bouncing off the low ceiling felt different from the party the night before. Here the stories being told were softly personal and laced with a lightheartedness borne of familiarity. I began to grasp that moments such as these carried the same meaning for families like the Whitcombes that morning waffle breakfasts had carried for me and my mother.

Katharine sidled up to me and in a low voice said, "You're doing a good job."

"A good job of what?"

"You're doing a good job of letting the moment come to you. Stay steady. It will come."

I wasn't sure what she meant, but I could guess. One of my co-workers at the accounting firm would call it "going with the flow."

I decided to go with the flow and say something to Katharine that would release what felt like a weight tied around my leg. "Katharine, I want to apologize for the way I reacted to you earlier."

She looked confused.

"In the entryway, when I was trying to leave."

"Che-che-che." With that and a slow blink of her eyes, all was pardoned.

Just then, Ellie swept into the room holding an oval platter with a perfectly browned turkey, complete with two white
chef's hats covering the ends of the drumsticks. Circling the
turkey was a wreath of fresh parsley, and spilling from its steaming cavern was dressing that bubbled with bumpy bits of apples,
cashews, and raisins.

"Well done!" Andrew spouted, clapping his hands.

"I hope it's not too well done," Ellie giggled. "Everyone, take
your place, please."

Julia climbed into her chair beside me. "Mummy, may we do
our crackers now?"

I looked around the table but didn't notice any crackers.
There hadn't been any with the appetizers, either.

Ellie placed the turkey platter in front of Edward's seat at the
head of the table and gave him a nod.

All of this fascinated me. I found these family traditions more
lovely and calming than I would have expected. There was a
system. A set of unspoken rules. Everyone knew his or her role.
This home was a place of order and steady rhythm. Never again
would I lambaste traditionalists and their conservative ways.
Done right, convention and form were irresistibly comforting.

Margaret sat at the head of the table on the other end. Ellie
sat in the middle, across from me and closest to the door. The
children, Andrew, Katharine, and I filled in the remaining seats.
The circle felt complete.

"All right. Shall we say grace then?" Edward asked.

I watched the others fold their hands and bow their heads.
Even Julia knew what to do. I was the last to lower my head but
did so willingly. Edward's respectful and warmly spoken prayer

captivated me. He had no difficulty addressing God with a reverent familiarity. He spoke his prayer of thanks much like a grateful son would speak to his father.

In this room, around this table, with these people, I found it easy to believe that God was listening to Edward's prayer. I also believed that some sort of significant first step had taken place between God the Father and me. I was accepted. I had been invited to come in. And I had entered under an eternal banner of grace and peace.

What remained to be seen was how the Whitcombes would respond once they knew who I was.

Chapter Twenty-Two

ay we do our crackers now? Julia asked as soon as her father finished the prayer.

"Yes. You first, Julia."

She reached for a paper party favor like the one each of us had by our china plates. The "cracker" was twisted at both ends, making it look like a large piece of wrapped candy. Julie held out one end to me. I never had seen a Christmas cracker before and had no idea what to do with it.

"You hold onto that end, silly," Julia said. "Then I pull like this."

With a loud snap and the scent of a snuffed match, the contents of Julia's cracker spilled onto the table. She picked up a folded piece of bright green paper, opened it, and placed the jagged paper crown on her head.

"Do you want me to read your riddle for you, Ju-Ju?" Mark leaned across the table eagerly.

"I can read it," she said.

"No you can't."

"Mark," his father said firmly.

We waited as Julia picked up a little piece of paper that had popped out of the cracker. It looked like a slip of paper from a fortune cookie, only wider.

She studied the message with great concentration. From where I sat, I could tell she had the paper upside down.

Jutting out her chin, she announced, "It's not very funny."

Everyone laughed.

Julia picked up the final prize from her snapping party favor. It was a small compass about the size of a thumbnail. She turned it this way and that and looked bewildered as to what it was or what she should do with it. Not willing to admit her befuddlement, she said brightly, "I was hoping it would be a tiny pony."

Everyone chuckled.

"Maybe I'll trade you." Mark took both ends of his cracker and gave it a good tug. Out of his cracker sprang a tiny top that landed on its point in the curve of his spoon and gave a "ta-da" spin before toppling over.

"Did you see that?"

"I'll trade, Mark." Julia quickly held out her compass. "But you should know I think this clock is broken because it keeps going wibbly-wobbly."

Mark placed his paper crown on his head and diplomatically said, "Let's see what everyone else gets first, Ju-Ju. Do you want me to read your riddle now?"

She handed it over, and Mark read to us. "What's black and white and read all over?"

"A newspaper." I hadn't heard that one for years.

"How did you know that?" Mark asked.

"I guess we have the same jokes in the US that you have here."

"Do your cracker now," Julia urged.

All the adults joined in, and a fabulous chorus of snaps around the table was followed by the rising scent of a snuffed match. To my surprise, everyone, including Margaret, placed the paper crowns on their heads. I played along and laughed as Andrew tried to read the small letters of his riddle without his reading glasses. He finally took Julia's route and announced, "It wasn't very funny."

We all compared our plastic toys. Mine was a ring that had a large pink "diamond." Julia was thrilled when I asked if I could trade her for her "watch." I told her I wanted a new watch for Christmas anyhow.

Our merry group was looking as silly as we could in our paper crowns when Ellie reminded Edward that the turkey was "going cold." He stood and began the grand carving of the Christmas turkey.

I looked down the table at Margaret. She appeared to be pleased with her son and his family. Everything felt idyllic. All that was missing was our own Tiny Tim and a rousing "God bless us, everyone!"

Katharine caught my eye and gave me one of her tranquil smiles. I held onto her calming expression all during the cozy meal.

We dined on turkey with dressing (or stuffing as the others called it), peas, and another surprising group favorite—steamed brussels sprouts. I found them to be as unexciting as the last time I had eaten them. But everyone else seemed to like them, including Julia.

The rest of the meal was delicious and the company delightful. I didn't join the cheerful conversation. It was so magnificent that I just wanted to sit back and be an observer. Aside from tiptoeing down the stairs with Julia just that morning, I had not fully entered into a moment of make-believe in years. Here, at this table, on this day, with these people, I found it easy to let myself slip into believing this was where I belonged.

I was buttering my last bite of dinner roll when Ellie said, "I hope you can forgive our company manners. We've been so chatty that we've barely included you in the conversation, Miranda. I do apologize. Please tell us about yourself. What part of the States are you from?"

"I live in San Francisco."

"My grandmother has been to San Francisco, haven't you, Grandmother?" Mark said.

"Regrettably, Mark, I have not been to San Francisco. I have been to California, but I visited Los Angeles, not San Francisco."

"Have you always lived in California?" Ellie asked.

"Most of my life."

"You weren't born in California, then?"

"No."

"Where were you born?" Mark seemed to like picking up his mother's lead and taking an adult part in the conversation.

"I was born in Michigan. But I wasn't there very long before we went to California." It felt odd inching into the topic of who I was and where I came from. Part of me wanted to blurt out the facts and be done with it. But this was the gentle route, Katharine's theory of "letting the moment come" to me. If this was going to be the truth-revealing conversation, then Margaret and her family deserved the gentle route.

Mark gave his plastic top a twirl again on his spoon. "Why did you go to California?"

"My mother had a job there."

"What did your mother do?"

"She was . . . she was an actress."

"My grandfather was an actress," Julia said.

"Ac*tor*," Mark corrected her.

"Ac*tor*," Julia repeated.

"What about your father?" Mark asked.

I swallowed, not expecting the question to come so blatantly. But then Mark expanded his question, explaining the reason for his curiosity. "Was your father an actor, as well?"

The answer, of course, was "yes," but I looked down at my hands and said, "I only lived with my mother."

"Why?" Julia asked.

I turned to Katharine, desperate to read in her expression that this was it. That the moment had come to me.

Without pause Katharine said, "Children, would you like to be excused from the table now? I would very much like to see what Father Christmas brought for you."

"Yes." Andrew rubbed his hands together.

"Andrew, I was asking the children if they would like to be excused."

"Right. I knew that. What do you say, Mark and Julia? Shall we go into the drawing room, and you can show us the presents Father Christmas brought you?"

"He brought me a tea set." Julia's eyes took on a sugarplum sparkle.

"How lovely." Katharine's expression made it clear that she was pleased with Julia's enthusiasm over the gift.

"Mummy," Mark said before pushing his chair back under the table, "what about the Christmas pudding?"

"I'll serve it in the drawing room a little later, all right, darling?"

Everything in me tightened as I anticipated the direction our conversation would go now that Katharine and Andrew were removing the small ears from the room. I felt uncomfortably hesitant to be the first to speak. It seemed there was no way to make this moment easy.

Margaret picked up the conversation thread. "My husband grew up without a father, as well. Professor Whitcombe was a casualty of World War I. My mother-in-law did an admirable job raising the two boys. But James often spoke of how difficult it was, not having a father around."

It touched me to know that my father had experienced his own measure of loss and heartache.

"I would imagine you experienced a few of the same challenges growing up without a father."

I nodded, trying hard to hold my thoughts and emotions in check. I didn't want to blow this. *If now is the time for me to say something, then please, God, let me say the right thing.*

"You said your mother was an actor." Edward leaned back and folded his hands.

"Actress," I corrected him, the way Mark had corrected Julia. I realized I had made the correction aloud instead of in my head, so I quickly explained, "She liked to be called an actress. Not an actor."

Edward appeared amused. "I now understand your comment at the party last evening when I told you my father was an actor. That line of work lends itself to a unique sort of position for the offspring, does it not?"

His sympathetic response to our shared life experience simultaneously consoled me and made the truth more difficult to speak. I hoped Edward would remember this brief moment of camaraderie once the facts were revealed.

"Did your mother perform on stage or in film?" Margaret asked.

"Stage."

I could feel my heart pounding.

"And is she still performing?"

"No, my mother passed away when I was eleven."

"Oh, Miranda, that's so sad. What a terrible shame." Ellie pressed her hand over her heart. "I'm sorry to hear that. Have you any brothers or sisters?"

I glanced at Edward and pressed my lips together.

"Oh, no siblings, either," Ellie concluded before I had a chance to speak. "That's really sad. How tragic to lose your mother when you're so young."

Edward leaned forward and asked a final question the way people do when they want to offer the freedom to speak honorably of the departed.

"What was your mother's name?"

This was it. I would not hop over the truth one more time.

I paused, drawing in a deep breath through my nostrils. The scent of bayberry from the candles made me nauseous. I knew that once I spoke her name, nothing in this room or in my life would be the same.

"My mother's name was Eve. Eve Carson, the actress."

The room went deathly still.

Chapter Twenty-Three

Margaret gripped the arms of her chair and stared at me without blinking. Her words came across the table like flat stones thrown into a still pond. Each word caused a ripple. Together they disrupted the entire ecosystem. "Eve Carson was your mother?"

I nodded, holding my trembling hands in my lap. I could hear Ellie exhaling the name "Eve," but I didn't dare look at her.

"Hold on there," Edward said, rising taller in his seat. "Are you trying to imply that your mother is the 'beguiling eve' in the poem?"

My throat tightened. I nodded. With dry lips I at last spoke the words. "I have reason to believe that Sir James Whitcombe was my father."

Edward pushed away from the table and stood up straight. Clasping his hands behind his back he said, "I am certain you are mistaken. And I must say this is not the sort of discussion I would have expected to take place in my home. Certainly not on Christmas and in the presence of my mother or my wife." Edward's scowl deepened. "I'm afraid I must ask you to leave, Miranda."

Stunned, I started to rise. My foot caught on my purse strap.

I remembered the picture and playbill and went for a last foray into the truth. "I'd really like to show you something before I go."

Edward clenched his jaw.

"Edward?" Ellie compassionately tilted her head.

Eye contact with his wife eased Edward's demeanor from blazing flames to slow-burning embers. Lowering into the chair he said, "What is it?"

I reached for the blue velvet pouch. Edward and Ellie seemed to recognize it as the purse that caused my panic when Julia brought it downstairs. Without an explanation, I handed the photograph to Edward.

The embers in his face were being fanned back into a flame. "Where did you get this?"

"From my mother's things."

He looked across the table at his mother and then back at me. "Why would your mother have this picture?"

"I think . . ." I glanced at Margaret and then down at the velvet pouch. This was so difficult. In a small voice I said, "I think perhaps my mother took the photo from your father. From his wallet. Many years ago. In Michigan."

"That proves nothing."

I slid the playbill across to him. "I was born nine months after this performance."

He glanced at the playbill and looked again at his mother. She stared across the table without blinking, her expression tightening into a pinch.

"Nothing here proves my father had any association with your mother. His name doesn't even appear on the playbill. You wouldn't have known about the 'eve' in the poem unless we had shown it to you—in confidence, I might add. I don't know what kind of a scam you're trying to pull on us, but I assure you, we will not fall for it. I believe you've had your opportunity to speak, and now I will once again ask you to leave."

Before I had a chance to point out the mention of the Society of Grey Hall Community Theatre on the playbill, Margaret let out a weighted sigh. Her lips moved as if she were talking in her sleep. "The play was *The Tempest*. Your mother performed the role of Miranda."

My heart did a flop. Margaret knew. She knew!

Edward checked the playbill and then stared at his mother. Ellie stared at me. Margaret wept silently. No one spoke.

I pushed back my chair and stood, ready to leave. Swallowing the tears that had puddled in my throat, I said, "Please understand. I did not come to England expecting anything like this to happen. My mother left only a few clues for me. The name of the studio on the back of the photo was what led me here. Yesterday, when I stumbled into the Tea Cosy . . . Well, it doesn't matter. All I want to say is I didn't plan any of this. You have all been very kind to me, and I want you to know that I never intended to hurt anyone. I'm sorry. I just . . . I just wanted to find my father."

That's when I broke down and cried.

"Miranda." Edward's voice carried the same gentle firmness that he used with his children. "Please sit down."

As I sat down, I tried to breathe, but all I could smell was the bayberry-scented candles.

"I can see how . . ." Edward took off his glasses and placed them beside his paper crown. The defeated prince sat with his hand covering his mouth, leaving his sentence unfinished.

Margaret produced a handkerchief from the cuff of her sleeve and used the rosebud end to blot her tear-moistened cheeks. With a wavering voice she said, "Miranda, it is clear—"

"Mother, if you don't mind, I would like to say something first." Edward cleared his throat. "I believe we can all appreciate your situation, Miranda. Losing your mother at an early age and not knowing the identity of your father are significant life obstacles. However, you must know that we are not novices when it comes to accusations and assumptions about my father. As he used to say, 'Such is the consequence of a touch of notoriety.' I may have reacted a bit too strongly in requesting that you leave. My apologies. We have all enjoyed your company. However, I must say I did not expect such an allegation to come from you."

"Edward."

"Just a moment, Mother. I have one more thing I would like to say."

He put on his glasses and looked more closely at me through the lower half. "The point is, you see, you have come to the wrong conclusion with, as you referred to them, the few clues your mother left you. I can guess at what you might have expected to gain from this, and yet I'm sure you can see how preposterous it is for you to expect any of us to—"

"No." I blinked away my unstoppable tears. "You don't understand. I don't expect anything from you. I don't even expect you to believe me."

"Then why have you brought all of this to the table?"

"I . . . I needed to find out the truth. And—"

"Well, the truth is that your mother may have had some slight association with my father and acquired the photo somehow. However, I'm afraid your search for your biological father cannot be resolved here."

"Edward," his mother said, her voice unnervingly calm, "I have something I must tell you."

I watched her words snuff out the fire from my half brother's face.

Margaret squared her shoulders and spoke in a resolute voice. "Edward, do you remember the summer you were twelve, when I took you and Marion to my parents' summer home?"

"Of course."

"That was the first time either of you had been with me to Sweden. Both of you kept asking when your father would arrive, and I told you he was working. What I didn't tell you, and never told either of you, was that your father and I were legally separated at the time. He had received an invitation from his colleague, Charles Roth—"

"Prospero," I said under my breath.

"Yes, Prospero." Margaret glanced at me and then returned her steady gaze to Edward. "Charles was cast for the role of Prospero. He had some sort of serious back injury a week or so before the play opened. That's when he phoned your father."

Edward looked down at the playbill. I knew he would see Charles Roth's name next to the role of Prospero.

"The playbills were already printed, you see, before your father decided to go to Michigan and take the part. All his life he spoke of that production as his favorite and his performance as his best ever. His only regret, he said, was that you children and I weren't there with him to see it."

Edward rubbed the back of his neck, slowly dissolving under his mother's confession.

"When your father returned to England that fall, we worked out our differences. Your father had been told that I was seeing someone while he was away. It was a lie. There was never anyone for me but James."

Margaret sighed and continued. "Many years later, perhaps you remember, your father had a bit of trouble with his heart."

"I remember," Ellie said softly.

"James believed his life was about to end. It was then he told me there had been a young woman. In Michigan. A very young woman. An actress. I've never forgotten her name. It was Eve. Eve Carson."

Edward leaned back in his chair, swallowing rapidly and holding his forehead. Ellie didn't move.

"Perhaps you can understand why I felt it was important never to speak of this to anyone. Edward, your father was a fine man." Margaret's voice trailed off as she turned to me and added, "He never knew . . ."

I tilted my head, wanting to grasp what I had just heard. "Are you saying he didn't know my mother got pregnant? He didn't know about me?"

Margaret drew in another breath for strength. "I can tell you this with absolute certainty. If my husband had known he had fathered another child, regardless of the circumstances, he would have searched day and night until he found you."

I swallowed the next wave of tears, dearly wanting to believe her words were true. The longing of my entire life was addressed in what this woman was saying to me—this woman who, of all the women in the world, had every reason to despise me.

With wobbling arms, Margaret pushed back her chair from the table. Edward rose quickly and strode across the room to help, but she was standing already. "If you will excuse me, I am going to lie down for a while."

"I'll walk with you to your room, Mother." Edward glanced over his shoulder at me before leaving the dining room. It seemed he wanted to say something, but he didn't. I didn't expect him to. Not yet. His expression made it clear he was processing all of this as best he could. In the meantime, his earlier request that I leave his house now seemed to be revoked.

Ellie and I sat across from each other, both speechless. I had the sense the two of us were cushioned together in a sort of soft, gauze-like silence.

Mark appeared in the doorway just then, announcing that he had come to see about the Christmas pudding. "It was Julia's idea, really. She wanted me to tell you she's ready."

"It will be a few more minutes, love. Tell the others for me, will you?"

Mark scampered off, and Ellie reached her hand across the table. I didn't know if she meant for me to reach for it or not, but I timidly stretched out my arm. She immediately gave my hand a squeeze.

I squeezed back.

Her smile floated across the table, making room for me in her heart the same way she had made room for me in her home.

"I feel so awful," I whispered.

"Oh, but you mustn't. It's going to be all right. You'll see. Give them—give all of us—a little time. That's all we need. A little time for this unexpected news to settle in. We'll come around."

I nodded hopefully.

"I knew there was something about you when I saw you last night. Now I know what it is. You have his eyes. Did you know that? You have your father's eyes. As clear as a blue sky on a spring morning."

Now it was Julia who burst into the dining room. "Mummy, Mark said I'm not allowed any pud because I didn't finish eating all my turkey!"

"You shall have your Christmas pudding, little love. Your brother is only putting you on. You just ignore him."

With a fist on her hip Julia declared, "But, Mummy, how can I ignore him? He's part of this family, you know?"

Ellie and I exchanged grins. "Well, Julia, he's not the only one who is part of this family, now is he? Every one of us has a place here."

I drew in the sweet implication of Ellie's words and held her blessing close. I was accepted. I, too, was part of this family. I belonged here.

"Mummy, will you please come and tell Mark that I get to have my Christmas pud?"

"Yes, yes, I'll come." Turning to me she added, "You will excuse me, won't you? I'll be back shortly."

"That's okay. I can start clearing the table."

"That would be lovely."

Julia grinned contentedly. Just before she left the dining room with her mother, she held up her hand to me with a twinkling grin. She wiggled her fingers so I would notice she was wearing the pink diamond ring I had given her from my Christmas cracker. I knew our friendship was sealed.

As I organized the plates and prepared to clear the table, my thoughts touched on all that had happened since I blew into Carlton Heath with the north wind on my heels. The sweetest impression that rested on me was that I was no longer alone. And not just because of the connection I now had with the Whitcombe family.

The attachment I sensed was larger than that. Something profound and abiding had happened in me at the heart level with Almighty God. He was the center of this celebration—the Father of Christmas past, present, and future. He had made himself accessible to me, to all of his children. I had responded, and now I belonged.

Reaching for one of the silly paper crowns, I placed it on my head and grinned at my reflection in the thick glass that covered the painting on the wall. I noticed in the reflection that someone else had entered the dining room. Turning toward the doorway I expected to see Ellie.

A new guest had arrived. A man about my age with a strong jawline and softly questioning eyes stood in front of me. He was wearing a tweed blazer over a black turtleneck. His light brown hair had a windblown look as if he had just arrived in a sports car.

"You must be Miranda," he said, rolling the "r" with the same Scottish twist that was so evident every time his father said my name.

I quickly pulled the paper crown off my head. "And you must be Andrew's son."

"Ian," he said.

"Ian," I repeated.

"So." He gave his earlobe a tug. "I heard you wanted to meet me."

"Really? The way I heard it, you're the one who wanted to meet me."

He smiled.

I smiled.

Both of us seemed to be turning a bit rosy.

I noticed Andrew standing just off to the side in the hallway. The jolly ole elf caught my eye and raised an eyebrow. I knew he was checking to make sure I liked the final gift he had just delivered on his rounds this year.

My answer to him was a great big bashful grin. I think he got the message. Ian certainly did.

That's when I realized the unimagined had happened. In my heart and in my life, it finally was Christmas.

Reading Group Guide

1. Do you know any women like Miranda who grew up without a father? How have these women filled the empty space in their lives?

2. What do you think of Miranda's decision to go searching for her birth father?

3. How did Doralee's spiritual experience affect Miranda in the long run?

4. Why do you think Miranda preferred to think of herself as an accident of nature rather than someone created by God?

5. Miranda liked accounting because the numbers could be "counted on" to always act in certain ways. What or who do you rely on to be stable when the rest of life seems to be on shifting sand?

6. How would you feel if you found yourself depending on the kindness of strangers at Christmastime?

7. What roles did the image of Father Christmas play in the book? In what ways was this "character" like God? In what ways was Father Christmas different from God?

8. Read Genesis 21:8-21. Ishmael was the son of a slave and of the slave's owner, Abraham. Early in life Ishmael was separated

from his father and raised by his mother. How do you think Ishmael felt about his father as Ishmael grew up? What do you think Hagar told her son about his father? Do you think she portrayed Abraham sympathetically or unkindly? What does this story tell us about fathers and mothers? What does it tell us about God as our heavenly Father?

9. Was there ever a time you felt your parents withheld important information from you, including possibly leading you to believe in Santa? How did you feel about your parents when you found out the truth?

10. Miranda was concerned that God might be like a one-eyed dragon on the other end of the swimming pool. Can you recount a time you thought of God as potentially dangerous? Did you, like Miranda, run away, or did you respond differently?

11. How did God win Miranda's heart? What does this tell us about him?

12. Can you recall a time someone beckoned you, like Christmas Present called to Miranda, "Come in, and know me better"? How did that make you feel?

13. What do you think of the way Miranda told the Whitcombes about her possible relationship to them? Do you think she handled the situation fairly for all involved?

14. What does the last paragraph of the book tell us has occurred in Miranda spiritually and emotionally?

15. Identify a time when you felt you were experiencing Christmas after a long winter in your life. How did that make you feel about God?

About the Author

Robin Jones Gunn grew up in Southern California, where both her parents were teachers. She attended Biola University and spent time traveling throughout Europe and attending Capernwray Bible School before marrying Ross Gunn in 1977.

Ross and Robin worked together in youth ministry for over twenty years and raised a son and a daughter while living in interesting places, including Reno and Maui.

When their children were young, Robin would rise at three a.m., make a pot of tea, and write pages and pages about her imaginary friends, Christy, Katie, and Todd. The Christy Miller series became Robin's first series of novels for teens, followed by the Sierra Jensen series. Over the past twenty years, Robin has written sixty-one books, including the bestselling Sisterchicks® novels for women, along with her award-winning gentle love stories in the Glenbrooke series.

For the past twelve years, Robin and her family have lived near Portland, Oregon, and are part of Imago Dei community. Robin loves to travel. She is a much-loved story-weaver and an aficionado of dark chocolate.

You are warmly invited to visit Robin at her Web site: www.robingunn.com.

If you liked

Finding Father Christmas . . .

Engaging
Father Christmas

Bestselling author Robin Jones Gunn brings readers another charming Christmas novella about a man and a woman, and a Christmas that just might change their relationship forever.

※

Miranda Carson's search for belonging continues in ENGAGING FATHER CHRISTMAS, the sequel to *Finding Father Christmas*. Arriving in Carlton Heath a year after her introduction to the charming community, Miranda is eager to visit the Whitcombe family but harbors doubts about how this Christmas will unfold. Will her relationship with Ian change everything for her and the Whitcombes? More important, how will Miranda respond when the engaging moment comes and Father Christmas is at the door?